LOVE STORY

(A SAILING BOAT)

SUNNY

Made with ♥ on the Notion Press Platform
www.notionpress.com

Contents

Prologue

The love journey of a boy **(Akash)** who gets into two serious relationships but ends up being separated from the love of his life. Despite having a good IQ level, a job, tremendous career-making decisions, and a supportive family, he couldn't find his inner self. His emotional and weak nature will be the cause of all the disturbances in his life. He worked hard to get everything on track, but a void in his heart remains forever.

CHAPTER ONE

'PREMATURE LOVE'

Most of the people in this world believe once they get a degree, life will be easy.

Complete myth!

The same was the case with Akash. He thought that practical life would be easy and everything would just work effortlessly on his end. It is a truth that no one prepared us for the real trials of life. But lucky enough, he was lucky enough to have a family that supports him emotionally as well as – maybe semi-financially. Akash has a good circle of friends but it doesn't matter who stands beside you when God plans to test you.

It was his result day. He was an average student who never fails in any exam but the result declaration time can make anyone nervous.

He opened his laptop with a trembling heart when his dad called him up to find out about his score on the final exam.

"Just open the website, my boy. I am with you," his father said on the phone that was on speaker

"Yes, Dad... let me check," he answered and clicked the 'enter' button. After a few seconds, his result card was in front of him.

"Hurrah! yes dad... I have done it," he screamed with joy.

"It's an A-grade," he added.

On the other side of the phone, his parents hugged each other with joy, with a genuine feeling of victory. No doubt parents are a blessing of God, who always celebrate our achievements as their own.

"I am proud of you, son..." his father said to him in a teary voice.

"When are you coming back home?" his mother asked.

"Soon mama... within hours. See you guys at dinner tonight,"

"Okay soon, we are waiting..." and then his parents said goodbye to him.

He was in the hostel to enjoy his last days with his friends, Rahul and Nikhil. After his result declaration, he went back home to Delhi and his family warmly welcomed him. They decorated the house with so many balloons and other decoration stuff. They both (His father and mother) decorated each corner of the TV lounge with all of their love. He was thankful to have parents full of life. It was the best day of his life. He hadn't seen his parents that happy before.

He had a loving and supportive middle-class family. They wanted him to study abroad, but he wasn't ready for that. He also shared his plan with his father about his higher studies. He wanted to live a less stressful life for a while because he knew that after getting into his professional life, he would ultimately become a stressful person. That's why he decided to enjoy this immature epoch of his life after his graduation. He decided to continue his higher studies after a break. So, his father agreed to his plan.

One day, he was having his breakfast when his phone beeped.

"One new message" on Facebook. He looked at the phone for a moment and shifted his focus again to his favorite homemade breakfast.

"Mom, should I tell you a secret?" he said with a smile to his mom.

"Of course son," his mother replies.

"You have magic in your hands. I just love your parathas" he was enjoying this breakfast after a very long time. He had an ideal family and Akash always was thankful to God for giving him such a supportive family.

After breakfast, he checked his phone and was surprised to read the sender's name on Facebook chat. It was Anshu from his school. Akash always wanted to talk to her but couldn't do so because of Anshu's attitude.

He used to like her but it was a one-sided love so he always ignored his feelings for her. He was not sure about Anshu's point of view. She was the most popular girl in the school and many boys used to like her. Akash, being an average-looking boy, was hesitant to talk to her.

He noticed her a few times, watching him in the school but he just took it as a coincidence. Today, her message on Facebook gave him immense pleasure.

He replied to her immediately. "Anshu from?"

She replied to him with a laughing emoji and he understood that she could imagine his condition.

"What about your college result?" the next message received.

Akash felt that he would die with happiness. He could sense that Anshu had stalked him, that is why she knew that he had just graduated from college.

"It was good. I got an A grade. What about you?" he replied with a smile. He was trying hard to act cool.

"I am good too. Also done with college and free nowadays" she replied.

After giving a brief introduction of their present lives they said goodbye to each other. They both hoped to talk sometime because at that time Akash had to leave the house since he had to attend a family function.

"Okay, we will talk again, I will wait" was the last message of their first conversation on Facebook, which Akash sent to Anshu.

"Me too" she replied, with a smiled emoji.

That day, Akash spent the whole day thinking about her. He was curious and wanted to know why Anshu texted him after a long time. What was the purpose of all of it? There were a lot of questions in his mind and he decided that he would talk to her on a phone call.

The next day, he sent a good morning message to her. After a random talk for an hour, he decided to ask her about a meeting.

"I remember that you are from Delhi. Where are you nowadays?" and he sent this message to her.

"Delhi" she replied. And Akash went crazy after knowing that she was in the same city.

"Can we meet now? Will she agree? Should I ask? Should I ask now, or after a few days?" Thousands of these kinds of questions started roaming in his mind. He was very happy but still, he was not sure if she would agree to meet or not.

"Hey, where are you lost?" Anshu messaged him when he was planning to ask, what to ask.

"Can we meet?" he sent her a message. He was waiting impatiently for the reply when the phone vibrated

"Sure" and Akash felt that someone had taken him into a fairyland where all his dreams would come true.

His next step was to ask about the day and her availability for the meeting. Akash had a lot of friends already; some of them were females but Anshu was her favorite one from school days. He felt something special for her. It was the reason behind all his excitement and Anshu's side of the story was untold till they met.

"Can we talk on the phone?" Being an obedient boy, Akash always used to ask for her permission before doing or saying anything to her because he didn't want to ruin this new friendship.

Akash and Anshu had no idea at that time what was in store for them. They were just affectionate with each other all of a sudden. Like all other teenagers, they weren't asking for anything except to make the present beautiful and memorable by loving and adoring each other. They were just thinking about the present, there was no long-term planning at that moment.

On one pleasant day, Anshu sent him a picture wearing a traditional Indian Lehenga. She was looking super-hot and beautiful in it. It was around 2 PM when he received the picture.

"Where are you going?" he asked at once.

He was planning a night out with his friends when Anshu's picture gave him goosebumps and he decided that he needed to meet her right now.

"At a family wedding. Am I looking good?" she messaged him.

"You are looking gorgeous. Can I come to see you right now?" he typed this message and sent it to her with a trembling heart.

"Are you insane? (With a laughing emoji) How can you come here? I am very far from your place." After receiving this message, he smiled for a minute and asked her about the location of the wedding venue.

They argued on the phone for a few minutes and then she agreed to send the location.

Akash canceled his plan with his friends and went to the wedding hall to meet Anshu. Before reaching there, he bought a very beautiful bouquet of red roses for her.

He went there and Anshu came to see him outside the hall.

"I was dying to see you; I hope you don't mind." He tried to convince Anshu that he liked her.

"I love you" he finally said while handing over the bouquet to her. She looked into his eyes for a second and then ran over to the hall with a shy smile on her beautiful face and she left for the hall.

Akash was a little confused that Anshu left without saying anything but happy that he finally said it.

"I love you too. I never thought that someone would do this for me." He received this message when Anshu disappeared from his sight. She probably tried to calm her down first and then sent him this message from the wedding hall.

That's how they confessed their feelings to each other. Akash went back to his home and called Anshu.

"I can't tell you how happy I am right now. Thank you for meeting me today." he thanked her on the phone call.

They talked till late at night and Anshu told him that she also liked his decent behavior from school days.

"Then why did you message me that day?" he asked.

"I used to stalk you very often and that day, I came to know about the completion of your degree. Then I thought to say hello to you because you are free now" she explained her side of the story.

"Oh, that's why you used to notice me in the school?" he questioned again.

"Yes," and they both laugh at each other.

"Hey, would you mind if I ask you to meet me again?" Akash asked her about a date.

"Don't worry, I will pick you up and drop you home before the night. I just want to see you again" he requested.

After explaining about his strict family, she agreed. They decided to meet at the weekend.

Anshu lived around 20kilometer away from Akash's house but the plus point for them was living in the same city. They both were very excited to meet. Now he has a commitment with Anshu. They were in a relationship and spent a lot of time on their phones. Akash's mother also noticed that he spent most of his time on the phone now. But as his father allowed him to take a break, no one asked him about his routine.

He started spending all of his time with Anshu because they were in love with each other so much. They used to express their feelings almost every day. During adolescence, adoring someone is more attractive than any other thing. They were waiting for their meet-up as well. It was hard for them to control their emotions at that moment because they never experienced them before in their lives. They considered their lives no less than a fairy tale at that period of life span.

The wait was over because the weekend had come. Akash was getting ready when his mother entered his room.

"Are you going somewhere?" she asked him politely.

"Yes, mom. I have a plan to meet some old friends today." He answered randomly.

"Great." His mother replies.

"Do you need anything?" Akash asks if she needs his help in anything but she refuses.

"Are you going to meet a girl?" his mother asked in a low tone. Akash looked at her with amazement. He was shocked, and his mother started laughing.

"Why are you laughing Mom?" he asked nervously.

"I was just thinking that my baby is now a grown-up boy," she said and left the room while smiling at him. She didn't even ask for an answer. Akash first thought that his mother knew all about Anshu but then he decided to talk to his mom when he got back.

All his focus was on the hairstyle, he was trying to make it look good for Anshu when his phone started ringing.

"Rahul Calling" the screen was lightning. He picked up the call.

"Hey, Aunt told me that you are going somewhere?" Rahul directly asked him a question.

"Why are you asking?" Akash counters-questions him.

"Is there any girl?" Both of them were playing a questions game when his mother stepped in.

"Hey, are you talking to any girl?" his mother asked.

"Hahaha… no mom, it's Rahul" he answered.

"Hey Rahul, say Hi to mom" Akash put the phone on speaker.

"Hi, aunt… it's me Rahul" Rahul said hi to Akash's mom and then she left the room.

"Akash, now tell me the truth" his best friend was now getting angry with him. He wanted to know about his plan but Akash requested him to wait till tomorrow. He agreed.

Akash got ready in an hour and left the home to meet Anshu. He picked her up from their chosen location and went for brunch.

Anshu was looking beautiful in a black frock with dark brown hair, covering her back. Akash adored her beauty with a red rose.

"I never thought that I could love someone this much" Akash confessed his love for Anshu once again. On reaching the restaurant, Akash opened the door for her and they entered the restaurant.

"What are your plans?" Akash asked her when they were having tea with some snacks.

"I want to continue my studies," she answered.

"That's great. I know that you are an ambitious girl. I remember how you always win the competitions" he explained.

"But you once defeated me in a writing competition," she said with a smile.

"Oh, you remember that?" Akash was a bit surprised.

They continue to talk about their school days for an hour. Then she told him about her madness for ice cream and at that moment, he asked her about her favourite flavor.

On reaching the ice cream parlor, they grabbed their favorite flavors and then went for a long drive.

Akash was enjoying every moment with her. Her presence made him feel good about life. Unexperienced by the hardship and hurdles of life, they were enjoying the best moments of their life.

"Would you mind if I held your hand?" Akash asked her when they were coming back home after a wonderfully perfect day.

She didn't even say a word. She placed her hand near Akash's hand on the car seat with a smile. Akash held her hand, and they continued to talk again.

Anshu was a bit of a dominative type girl but she also liked him very much. Over time, they started to plan their future together. Akash had told his friends Rahul and Nikhil about his relationship with Anshu and they both were in their support. But Akash's parents still had no idea about all this.

One day, they talked for an hour on the phone. Anshu was missing him badly when she sent a message to him after a few hours of disconnecting the call "What about a coffee date today?"

Akash was also getting bored at home when her message gave him plenty of happiness in one second.

He got up immediately and went to meet her. She wore an orange shirt paired with blue jeans and silver hoops in her ears. She was looking ravishing in that attire. Akash was fond of her dressing sense. She was dressed up to the nines.

It was a pleasant day, and the temperature was also in control.

She tied up her hair in a bun.

"You are looking handsome" Anshu gave him a compliment for the first time in their relationship and Akash was holding her hand even tighter than before. He was an average-looking guy but the glow of being with the right person and the feeling of being loved can make anyone look more beautiful than ever.

They went to a coffee shop and Akash gave her a beautiful rose. Giving a rose to Anshu had become a mandatory part of their dates. They were talking with each other when Rahul stepped into the coffee shop and stopped near them.

"Hey, what a coincidence!" he became so happy and moved forward his hand to greet Akash. Akash and Anshu were also happy to see him here.

Rahul said goodbye to them after a brief introduction and the lovebirds continued to adore each other. In the meantime, the waiter served their coffee, and they received it while staring each other in the eyes.

Life was going very smoothly for them. They used to spend time with each other, go on dates, send pictures to each other, lovey-dovey gifts, and long phone calls at night.

Everything was going well until one day Akash came to know that Anshu was planning to go to Australia for higher studies.

"But you never told me before that you want to go abroad for higher studies?" They were continuously arguing.

"How can I tell you a plan that just happened? I told you that..."

And Akash disconnects the call. He was very angry at this sudden decision to go abroad.

"You have to discuss everything with her in detail" Rahul tried to calm him down when he came to know about the situation. Rahul came to see him when he talked about their fight.

It was quite normal to have a fight and a light argument, but the thing that disturbed Akash the most was Anshu's behavior. She didn't even try to convince him with love. But Rahul kept insisting on him that he should call her.

After three days Akash called Anshu. She was crying at the call.

"Are you all right?" Akash forgot about his anger and asked about her.

Then she said that she was worried about their relationship. She thought that it was going to end soon and that Akash would never talk to her again.

"I am sorry, I love you ... I can understand that you have ambitions and I don't want to fight with you again" Akash tried to relax her.

They talked again and after discussing the whole situation in detail, they decided that Anshu should go to Australia.

"If you want to pursue your dreams, I will never become a hurdle for you. I will wait for you" he confessed his pure feelings for her.

"I am sorry, I should have talked to you about it earlier," Anshu said.

Everybody says that you don't need to say "sorry or thank you" to anyone in any relationship, but the truth is, these two words can save any relationship.

One sorry with a pure heart can make a big difference. The same case happened to them. They started to talk again and Akash kept on supporting her again.

After a month, Anshu went to Australia and they met for the last time before her departure.

It was a cool breezy day. They were sitting in a restaurant when she held his hand and said "I want you to take care of yourself. Promise me that you will focus on your future and then we will be together soon" Akash was very sad but he managed to smile.

"I promise." He looked at the coffee cup and took a pause.

"I will miss you," he added.

"Look, I have got something for you" She opened her bag and gave him a teddy bear.

"I want you to look at it, whenever you miss me. I know it's going to be hard for us but I have full confidence in you." She gave him the teddy bear and looked at him.

"Doesn't it look like you?" she was trying to make him laugh.

"No, I think it looks like you" he replied and they both laughed.

"We have many different apps to talk to. Facebook, Skype, and OH yes, I want you to send me emails every week" Anshu was trying to change his mood.

"And you will send me your pictures, with cute and funny faces. Promise?" he asked with a sad face.

"My face is funny?" she laughed.

"Yes, very funny. You are my cartoon." He finally laughed

"Hahaha... only your cartoon" she replied.

"You know what, I can be a cartoon, for this cute smile," Anshu said with a wink. He kissed her hand.

They spent a few hours together and did some shopping. Akash gave her a goodbye kiss and dropped her home.

She had a flight two days after their last meeting. She sent a photo to Akash with the traveling bag she packed for her.

"Stay safe darling," he replied.

"Let me know when you reach Australia" he sent a second message.

They used to talk every day when Anshu reached Australia. Akash started missing her very much, so Rahul suggested that he should start a job.

"You have to start doing something productive. It is not good to ruin your golden time by sitting idle." Rahul succeeded in convincing him and he applied for a job in his city.

His parents were very glad about his decision. He called Anshu at first and told her about the confirmation of his new job.

"I am very happy for you. Now you don't have to miss me every day" She was genuinely happy for him. And the call disconnects due to a network issue.

"Keep me informed about your day. I am going to class now. Have a good day" Akash received this message and replied to her with a smile.

"Just ask me if you need any help or guidance" his father tries to boost his confidence on his first day.

"I know he can rock the office game" his mother kisses his forehead with pride on her face. He changed himself a lot after Anshu left Delhi.

He then stepped out of the house towards his office with the hope of a better future.

'THE HARDSHIPS'

"So, it was a brief introduction about our company. I hope you will learn all the other tactics with time. Wish you good luck" The tall, handsome, and decent man was standing in front of Akash, giving instructions to him on his first day.

"Let me show you your room, sir," he asked Akash to follow him and they both went towards a hallway.

Akash spent the whole day checking the files and trying to understand his tasks. He didn't get any time to contact Anshu or even send a message to her. At 6 PM he grabbed his laptop bag and dialed Anshu's number while sitting in his car in the parking area. She didn't respond.

"Where are you?" He left a message for her and started the car. His home was a 30-minute drive away from the office. He was happy and excited about his first day and badly wanted to share it with her, but she was busy. After an hour, he received a notification from her account. She had posted a picture with her foreign friends hanging out late at a mall. Akash becomes very angry.

Late at night, she tried to call him but he was sleeping because he was very tired.

She called again in the morning. "Where were you?" she asked.

"I tried to call you several times, but you were busy with your friends. I think they are more important for you now" his tone was very bitter.

"Hey, what are you saying? Are you out of your mind? You better know who is important and who is not!" she tried to clarify her position.

It was the first argument between them, that was a little harsh and they continued to argue for about 30 minutes.

"You can send me a message before going out or you can inform me about your schedule" he was very angry with her.

"I thought it was your first day, and you are in the office so I didn't find It appropriate to call you" she was giving justifications.

"Whatever Anshu..." he answered.

Anshu tried to calm him down but all in vain.

"Okay, check your email. I have sent you something" she said during the call and when Akash opened the mail, it was a picture.

He smiled. "I know that you are smiling..." she said to him. The phone was on speaker mode and he was lying on his bed.

"No, I am not smiling..." he takes a pause.

"I am blushing," he said with a burst of laughter, and after a lovey-dovey romantic phone call conversation, he hung up the call and got ready for the office.

"Have a good day" he received a message before leaving the house. He smiled at the phone and at the same time, his father noticed him.

"Is there anything funny in it?" he asked with a mischievous smile.

"No Dad, it's just a random notification. Okay, I am leaving, see you guys at dinner" and he grabbed the keys and left.

It was his second day. He was already missing Anshu, so he sent a text message to her. While waiting for the response, he was trying hard to control his temperament.

It was the new job and a new routine that was making him crazy and temperamental. Anshu's behavior and carelessness were working like icing on the cake. Due to their busy schedules and not being able to talk with each other, they started to have differences.

That day, they had a bitter argument again. Both spend the whole week in frustration with each other.

At the weekend, they decided to do a Skype call and talk about everything in detail.

"Hey, you are looking weak and sick." Anshu inquired about his health at first when the call time started.

"That's not the case. It's just, I had a tough week. I get used to the routine with time" Akash answered.

Then they talked about their busy routine and gave justifications to each other for not being responsive on time.

"I think it's better to find a solution to all these issues, rather than blaming each other" Anshu suggested a way out to make their relationship work.

They set some specific hours to talk, and promise to focus on their work/study the rest of the time.

Days passed by and things got better with time. It's been 6 months since Akash joined the office. He was performing well at the office and their relationship was also going great.

"Let's video chat" Anshu received this message from Akash when they were texting on Facebook.

"Right now?" she asked with excitement.

"Yes, right now. I want to see you" they replied.

"But you have a working day tomorrow, and it is very late now" She again tried to confirm whether he wanted to or just asked as a formality.

"You are more important to me" he replied and Anshu's heart skips a beat. She smiled stupidly. She opened his laptop and answered the video call. It was 2 AM and both of them were in their nightdresses.

"You are getting prettier day by day" he compliments her first.

"Because I am very happy, and that's all because of you and your love" she gave him a sweet reason for her glow.

"Do you have any plans to come back during these summer vacations?" Akash asked about her plans.

"Yes, maybe... I will talk to my parents first and then will decide about it" she answered.

"Great. I will be very happy if I get the chance to meet you soon" he said to Anshu while his eyes were on the laptop.

'Hey, look at me... are you missing me?" Anshu wants to know but Akash just smiles in return.

"How's your office? Or do you need anything from Australia?" she asked.

"Yes, I need you" he answered, but this time with a wide smile on his face. They started laughing and one of Anshu's room-mates woke up.

"Please turn down its volume," she said in her sleepy voice. Anshu looked at Akash and they both laughed at her because she thought that Anshu was watching a movie and that's why she asked her to turn down the volume.

It was 1 AM, and Anshu didn't have a headset. Her laptop was on full volume.

"You know what? I always think about you in my office, and whenever I call you, you never pick up my call. Now tell me one thing honestly, am I wrong if I get angry after all of this fuss?" he stopped for a moment.

"Look Anshu, I have a lot of things here to deal with! Especially after joining the office... and if we continue to fight every few days, things will be more difficult to handle," he was trying to make her understand that it is not possible to have a perfect and ideal relationship all the time. Everyone has to make some compromises to make things work.

Though he was not mature enough, he was behaving like a responsible guy at that moment. Every relationship has its weak points, and we just have to work on them to keep going.

Anshu, being the only child of her parents, was a little spoiled and a bit more arrogant but it was true that she loves Akash. She was also trying to make this relationship stronger but her childishness and carelessness were destroying everything.

That night, Akash tried his best to make her aware of the fact that she needed to be a bit more responsible and mature. Deep down in his heart, Akash knows that her friend circle and the environment of an advanced country have affected her mind.

She was a bright student, that's why she got admission on scholarship but her present performance in exams was unsatisfactory.

She used to hang out now and then with her friends. Akash even scolded her badly for not doing well in exams and they again had a fight that lasted a week.

"I always thought that you would be happy to see my pictures with my friends but you always do this" she replied to him when they were arguing over her result.

"I want to see you happy Anshu, that is why I am worried about your result. You didn't score well and the sole reason for this poor result is your friends and then your irresponsible behavior."

"So, you are trying to control me?" Anshu screamed at him.

"Am I trying to control you? Don't you have a mind of your own?" he shouted back at her. They were arguing on the video call when one of Anshu's friends entered the room.

"Is everything all right?" she asked.

"Yes, I am fine. Just leave me alone" Anshu replied to her and she went back.

"Why is she interfering in our personal matters?" Akash was very angry.

"She just comes to check on me," Anshu replies.

"Anyways, I want you to change your routine, and be more serious about your studies." He was still on his point.

"Stop acting like my parents Akash. I am not a child and I know what is good for me and what is not." She said this aloud and disconnected the call by shutting down the laptop at once.

Akash got very angry with her. He didn't even call him for two days and then discuss the whole situation with Rahul. He makes him understand that whatever she does, you have to call her once. Akash did the same.

He called her on the third day but she didn't answer. He sent her many messages but got no response. A week passed like this and he got no calls from Australia.

On the 8th day after their fight, his phone rang. He was in the meeting. Being unable to attend the call, he becomes frustrated and leaves the meeting to call her back after 10-15 minutes.

"Where were you?" she almost screamed.

"I think I should ask this question. Where were you from the last few days?" he questioned her directly.

"I was busy with my studies," she replied coldly.

"And why did you call today?" he questioned again. He was acting heartless but he was right.

"Because I was missing you." Her confession failed to melt his heart this time.

"Where are you? And do your friends know that you called me today? He tried to inquire about something.

"I am at a restaurant for dinner. No one is with me" she answered politely this time.

"I knew it. Tell me the truth, do your friends stop you from talking to me?" he was trying to find the reason.

"What are you saying, Akash? why would they do that?" she becomes nervous.

"I know that your friends told you so." He said aloud.

"And you are stupid enough to believe in them" he added.

"How dare you, Akash? You are right. She told me that you are an ordinary guy with a sick mentality who tries to control his women" she screamed.

"What did you just say???" Akash can't believe his ears. His heart broke into pieces. His stupid Anshu is in the control of those ill-mannered foreign girls.

"You heard it right. I am just sick of your controlling behavior. I am here to enjoy my life on my terms, and not on yours." She was shouted on the call.

"But I always tried to give my best to you and this relationship" Akash's voice was becoming teary. He couldn't believe that a girl could do this, and the worst part was it was his girl. His Anshu- His school time love.

Sometimes people can do more damage to you, by being with you. And then you realize that it's better to just miss them than to be with them and hurt yourself every day. Akash's condition was almost the same.

He was unable to speak after listening to all of her thoughts about his personality and character. He knows that Anshu is an irresponsible and childish girl, but he never thought that she had this kind of view about his mentality.

While standing on the balcony of his office, he was feeling the broken pieces of his heart in his chest. There was pain, there was sadness, there was grief and sorrow of being left alone- of being separated from the love of his life. He has planned his future with this girl and now it is very hard to believe that he has to live without her.

Anshu was screaming something on the phone, against him and his mentality... but he was unable to listen. Everything on the planet Earth just stopped for him. All he was listening to was the voice of some shattering pieces of his heart.

"I want to be free now, and I want to end this toxic and controlling relationship" He manages to listen to Anshu's voice for a second and all he listens to are her rude sentences over this relationship.

"Toxic?" Akash only said this in return for her objections.

"Yes, toxic. You always argue with me for not attending your calls. I can't be your robot anymore?" She takes a pause.

"I called you today, just to give one last try to our relationship. But you, all men, can't change." Her voice was cold.

"It's over, Akash... I am sorry I can't do this anymore." And the phone call disconnects forever.

He didn't even get a chance to say a word. She didn't even ask about his side of the story. Why does he become rude to her? It was a sad and unexpected day for him.

It is not true that all men are the same. Some are very sensitive and just want loyalty from a girl, but we are all pawns in the hands of destiny.

Saying goodbye to someone you've given your heart and love to, whether you've been together for a few weeks or several years, is the worst thing ever and Akash has to go through this.

He just sits on the balcony having flashbacks from their meetings and how they used to hold hands. A drop of tear appeared at the edge of his right eye. It was full of pain and sorrow.

He spends the next hour sitting idle on the balcony. One of his colleagues noticed that he was in trouble. He talked to him and advised him to take a leave. His boss allows him to go home.

"Can you come home right now?" he messaged Rahul while coming back home. Rahul lives in the same block so he was in his room when Akash returned home. His eyes were sore and the temperature was high.

"Are you all right?" His parents were not at home so Rahul attended to him. He just hugged him and talked about his last call with Anshu.

It was hard for Rahul too, to believe in all this. He was also very surprised to know about the thinking of such an intelligent and modern girl.

"You should explain...." Rahul was about to say something when Akash stopped him.

"Rahul please, I don't want to talk about this anymore... I am just a little hurt, that's why I called you" he was continuously staring at his hands when he said this.

"Being judged wrong by your favorite person is the worst feeling ever... you just feel helpless, like I am feeling right now" He explained his feelings to his best friend, whom he could rely on.

Even when a relationship is no longer healthy, a divorce or breakup may be excruciatingly painful since it signifies the loss of not only the partnership but also the shared ambitions and commitments. Romantic relationships start on a high note of anticipation and desire for the future. When a relationship ends, we are left with feelings of betrayal, tension, and loss.

Akash was going through hell, and he did not know what Anshu was feeling right now. This thing was disturbing him very much. He wants to talk to her, to know about her feelings. But Akash can't do so. This pain and disruption were killing him.

On the other hand, Anshu was also very sad. Her friends were helping her, but in true meaning, they were just dictating her.

"Don't stifle your emotions. It's natural to experience numerous ups and downs and to experience a wide range of emotions, including anger, resentment, grief, relief, fear, and confusion. It's critical to recognize and acknowledge these emotions." Her friend was trying to make her calm when she was weeping badly.

"You are a strong girl, Anshu. Keep in mind that the ultimate goal is to move on. In some ways, expressing your sentiments will release you, but you must be careful not to concentrate on unpleasant feelings or over-analyze the circumstances. Stuck in negative emotions like blame, wrath, or resentment saps your vitality and prevents you from healing and going forward." One of them holds her hand and tries to make her realize the real facts of life.

But the problem here was different. All of them were manipulating her mind.

"Have you ever thought, why does he never contact you again after your call?" one of them asked.

"Because I stopped him, I warned him to never contact me again," Anshu replied while crying badly.

"No, he did so because he is happy without you" her friend answers as if she knew everything about Akash.

The biggest mistake Anshu made was to believe in her stupid friends and their opinions about her man. It was a common mistake that we all made in our teenage love- to believe or to listen to a third person except our partner.

When you allow someone to invade your personal space, and talk about your matters with theirs, ultimately people ruin your relationship. And the second mistake that Anshu and then Akash made was to stop fighting for their love.

A relationship is a very beautiful feeling and it means effort. The entire concept of a relationship is to be accepted, nurtured, accepted, and believed in. When one fails to do so, he/she becomes the actual cause of the breakup.

In simple words, every relationship works on some terms. People feel shy to speak about it, but the truth is, you can't expect something to work properly when you stop working on it. The problem with Akash and Anshu's relationship was their age. It was a premature love, that we can call only affection. The affection of that age, to be loved and to be appreciated. If it was not only a simple affection, Anshu would surely try her best to make it work but she didn't do so. Why?

This "why" was also disturbing Akash badly. He wants the answer to his few questions: why did she allow someone to dictate or predict their relationship but after a few days, he changed his focus. Rahul tries his best to show him the bright side of life. In a nutshell, he proves to be his real friend.

His mother also has an idea about what is going on, but she never wants to disturb him.

One day she calls Rahul in the absence of Akash. "You have to tell me the truth. What has happened to him and why is he behaving so rudely with everyone?"

"You guessed it, right aunt. He is going through a tough time because of a girl... "and then he narrates the whole story to his mother.

"Is he performing satisfactorily at his office?" she asked about Akash.

"Not sure, but I think I should visit his office someday... if you want me to do so," Rahul explained.

"Yes, please..." she ordered him to take care of Akash because he only listens to him.

Akash was a sensitive boy, which is why he took a long time to come back to his normal life. His mom knows everything about his relationship and her ultimate goal was to bring him back to normal life.

"I was planning a trip together..." her mother said one day at the dinner table.

"Trip? Together?" Akash was the first one to respond to his mother's idea.

"Yes, a family trip for all of us," she said while looking at each member of his family.

"That's a great idea actually," Akash replies. He always pretends that he is all okay but his mother knows that he always hides his problems.

"But on one condition" Akash added after a few moments when he was about to swallow the bite of his favourite chicken steak, his mother always cooks specially for him.

"What is it?" This time, his father was the one to take part in the conversation.

"I will sponsor this trip," Akash said with pride in his eyes- for his family and for being an independent guy who can take care of his family.

"Ahh, what a wonderful day it is. I am in" his father said with a roaring voice- of a proud father.

"Done. I will finalize the destinations" his mother said excitedly and the whole table laughed at once. What a happy family!

They all planned the perfect family trip for the next few days and left for their destination at the weekend.

Before leaving for the trip, he received a message from his best friend- Rahul that reads:

"Message: Accept what is, let go of what was, and have faith in what will be. We all love you."

While reading this message from his best friend, he eyed his mother who was very excited to spend time with his family, and he felt like the luckiest person alive.

His immature love came to an end but, his forever love for life has just started.

CHAPTER THREE

'LOVE DEPARTURE'

Akash was sitting at a hill station with his family, having his favorite black coffee. He didn't like black coffee at first, though he was fond of tea, and now he has become addicted to bitterness. He loves to have simple aromatic tea in winter but this Akash is a new one.

"What are your plans, son?" His father asked. They were out for lunch on their first day of the trip.

"I didn't think that much about the future..." he replied.

"For god's sake, we are here to enjoy" his mother interrupts him.

"Hahaha..." Akash just laughs at their sweet gestures.

"No more stressed discussions" she added, as she warned her husband and son.

They were sitting like a happy family but the truth is, one has a broken heart (Akash), one has a stressed mind (father) and one has a tensed heart (mother). Things didn't always run smoothly and we never knew the truth.

It's impossible to get everything exactly how you want it. There are just too many other variables at play, the most important of which is what other people want. We all have competing wants and needs, and our desires are frequently hindered when they clash with those of others.

They spent a whole week in the hills, pretending to be the happiest persons alive but in the end, everyone has to face the bitter realities of life. You can't escape from your responsibilities for a long time.

Just like that, they had to leave that hill station and come back home with the same daily grind of life.

Akash was trying to learn how to live with the flow of life instead of going against it. His mother was helping him secretly.

The day they came back home, Akash was feeling a little lighter. It can be seen through the calmness on his face. Every day he began to feel significantly less stressed as if a burden had been lifted from his shoulders.

He went straight to meet Rahul in his house.

"Hey champ, how are you?" Akash greets him warmly.

"Woo ho...what a change!" Rahul hugged him.

"Hahaha... I am forever fresh" Akash said with a wide smile.

"Look who's talking..." Rahul laughed.

They met like forever best buddies.

"Akash?" Rahul said with a serious tone. They were having a chit-chat at tea.

"I am glad that you are looking happy..." Rahul looked at his eyes. Akash smiled.

"After ages" Rahul added.

"I know what you are trying to say. It's okay, go on..." Akash makes him comfortable.

"I just wanted to say that you are doing great. I am glad that you moved on. She doesn't deserve you. Destiny has a plan for you" he looked at Akash's eyes. The pain was everywhere.

"Okay let's forget about it! What about the office?" Rahul asked politely.

"Umm... yeah... I will join again tomorrow." He replied.

"Great. It means that you are free today?" Rahul asked again.

"Yes, no special plans. Why are you asking?" Akash wanted to know about the plan.

"Let's go swimming" Rahul seemed excited.

"Hahaha. Are you serious?" Akash laughed.

"I remember our college days. How you always laugh after throwing me in the pool" and they laughed.

They chit-chat for an hour and get ready to rock at the swimming pool. Akash always succeeds in cheering him up.

After spending a good day with Rahul, Akash went back home. The next day at the office, he came to know that the company had hired some new employees and there was a welcome party in the evening.

Being the youngest one and an excellent performer at the office, Akash was appointed as a supervisor to all the newcomers.

His boss gave him brief instructions on how to train the new staff.

"I know that your performance was questionable at one time, but you had a good comeback. I am glad that you have the potential to deal with a tough time. That is why I choose you to supervise the new staff. It's good for you to meet new people and learn from them" This was the message his boss said to him.

"Pleasure is all mine sir. I will try my best" Akash replies.

In the meeting room, Akash gave his brief introduction to all the trainees and let them know about the company and its rules. All the trainees were young and determined.

"Sir, I think you are a strict boss. I mean a serious one." One of them said aloud in a friendly manner.

"You guys have to behave professionally on the premises of this office. Otherwise, strict actions will be taken against you." Akash kept quiet for a second after saying this.

"And yes, I will be a strict boss if you guys behave like this," he added.

"Sorry, sir" the over-friendly boy apologised.

Then he professionally starts the meeting. That average-looking boy looked confident and handsome today. Pain indeed changes you. Some unexpected events in life can change your perspective of life, but on the other hand, if we try to look at the brighter side of life, it is very beautiful in its way. We just have to discover those ways- to look and deal positively.

Akash, with the help of his friends and loving family, was also trying to look at the brighter side of life.

"Sir, if we need any help regarding the projects assigned to us, to whom we can contact?" One of the girls from the new badge asked this question from Akash when he was busy collecting his files at the end of the meeting.

"Good question. My email and contact number will be shared with all of you. You can contact me or Miss Sadaf (his colleague) whenever you want" he answered and left the room.

Akash was working on his laptop that same day when a reminder of Anshu's birthday popped up on the screen. He immediately canceled it and tried his best to concentrate again on the work, but his mind was disturbed now. Meanwhile, a group of newcomers knocks at his door.

"Yes, come in" he allows them to enter.

"Hello sir, I am Nisha," one of them introduced herself.

"I am Rishi" a boy introduces himself

"And I am Shree" the third girl also introduced herself.

"Sir, we are sorry to disturb you but we need a little bit of help... just guidance for our project" Shree continued.

"Sure, please sit" he welcomed them and then discussed the project completely.

After an hour when they were about to leave, Akash suddenly remembered that he was thinking about Anshu but their presence and the workload helped him to get rid of all his disturbing thoughts. He smiled, collected his belongings from the table, and went back to his home.

He was having dinner with his family when his phone rang. An unknown number was calling. He ignored the call because it was family time and he didn't want any interruption in it.

After having dinner, he checks his phone for a while and then goes back to sleep.

The next day in the office, he asked about the project from all the newcomers. Some of them have performed well, but there were a few whose projects were incomplete.

Akash scolds them and when one of them tries to give a justification, he orders them to keep quiet. After the meeting, Shree knocks at the door.

"Yes, come in..." he asked her to sit.

"If you are here for any extension, then I am sorry. You should have told me earlier about it" he was very angry.

"But sir... I have called you many times, but you didn't respond" she answered.

"You called me for the project? When?" he becomes so shocked that he scolds her without any reason.

"Sir I tried to call you yesterday, to let you know about the project but you have not answered my calls" She shows him her phone, and then Akash checks his phone too. She was right. Damn. "How could I miss a call? Oh, it was family time and I ignored it." He thought.

"Okay, I am sorry, but you have to message me... I don't know that's it's you" he tried to handle the situation.

"No, sir it's okay... I will complete the project today once you brief me on the method" she answered efficiently.

"Okay great." He replied.

"If any other employee needs help, then please call them." He said politely.

"Sure sir," she answered.

She called two other employees and Akash briefed them about the project. The next day, everyone performed well in the meeting in front of higher authorities, and C.E.O and Akash were appreciated for training the staff.

On one fine day, Akash was out of his office for a tea break and when he entered, Shree was there waiting for him.

"Hello sir," she said with a smile.

"Sir, I am here to thank you for helping me with the project." She added.

"Oh! That's not a problem. It's my duty" he replied humbly.

They talked with each other for half an hour because Akash finds her a well-raised girl but he still feels uncomfortable with every girl he meets.

Shree noticed his reserved behavior, especially with girls. Sometimes he also becomes rude to girls but no one knows the actual reason behind it.

Rahul once called him at night and informed him about his meeting with Akash's mother.

"But why didn't you tell me this before?" he was surprised to know that his mother knew everything about his past relationship.

"So, you are saying that mom knows everything?" Akash's tone was very harsh.

"Yes," Rahul took a pause. "She is your mother, Akash. She was worried about you. You were behaving very weird that's why she called me and I promised her to take care of her son" he explained.

After a lighter argument, Akash got his point.

"You know what, I hate you," he said with a smile and pride on his face. He was feeling blessed to have such pure and lovely people in his life.

"Hahaha... but I love you my boy" Rahul laughed at his sweet anger.

The majority of the people in this world have gone through tough times, but a few of them have the power to surpass that hard time with courage and patience. And very rare ones seem to be better able to cope in those difficult times.

It is a very wise saying that you have to go through the worst to become the best. Akash's life was like that. His capability to overcome the negativity of this life was remarkable. Although he still feels hesitant with girls, just because of one girl. He was not wrong there.

Shree noticed his behavior in the office. She once called him, when he was about to sleep. She wants to discuss some random things about their project. They have become colleagues now.

"I hope that I have not disturbed you," she said politely.

"No, it's fine. Please go on" and then they talked for an hour. Akash feels that she is not like other arrogant girls. That was the only reason he used to talk with her quite often.

One day, Akash was about to leave the office when he saw Shree waiting for a cab.

"Hey, please come. Let me drop you home" he stopped his car near her and asked her to get in the car.

"No thanks, sir... I am just waiting for..." she was about to complete when Akash interrupted her.

"No, formalities, please. Get in the car" This time he was a little serious. Shree can't refuse so she gets in.

"I have to do some grocery shopping for my home, that's why..." Akash again interrupted her.

"That's not a problem. I also have to go to the mall" he said with a cool smile.

He recently came to know that Shree is the only breadwinner of her family and her father had retired. She was a well-raised girl and very much younger than him, so he started respecting her.

"Tell me something about your family..." he asked while driving.

"I have a younger sister. She is studying. And a mother... who is a housewife" she replied.

"Oh right..." he replied

"You know what... I don't have a sister. And I don't know how to shop with the girls." They laughed at his confused gestures.

"Hahaha... that's not a problem sir." She said while trying hard to control her laughter.

They did shopping for Shree's house and then he requested her to meet her mother.

"Sure sir" and she agreed.

Akash and Shree went to his house to meet his mother. She was a simple woman.

"Hey mom......hello.....where are you? Oh, there you are." His mom was watching television and did not hear them coming. "I have a friend from the office who came to see you." pointing towards Shree.

"She is Shree, my friend from the office. She is like my little sister."

From that day, they became good friends.

"I want to ask something if you don't mind," Shree said one day to him when they were out for lunch.

"Yes," he answered very randomly while taking a sip of fresh orange juice.

"Do you have a girlfriend?" And suddenly the orange juice becomes the world's most bitter juice ever. Akash took a deep breath and smiled.

"Yes. Her name is Shree and she is my sister" and then he laughed hysterically. Tears start to appear in his eyes.

"You.... are very funny," he said while laughing. Shree feels that he is not normal.

"Okay, I will not ask again. You can tell me frankly if you don't want to talk about it" she said with genuine care in her eyes for Akash.

"No, you are getting me wrong," he explained.

"Her name was Anshu...." And then he talked about his relationship after a long time. Now, he was strong enough to talk about this.

Here strong means that Akash understands what it's like to be weak, helpless, and exhausted by life's trials and tribulations, yet he still gets up every morning hoping for a better day. He was still optimistic about the future. Even when he is exhausted, he digs out what's left of his energy and keeps going because he believes things will eventually change.

That's what he was trying to do. He just spent time with others, who needed his time and energy. That's why he chooses Shree, a deserving, weak girl to take care of.

He ultimately understands that after being beaten down over and over again, there is power in getting back up and fighting with the world.

He knows that despite the world shoving your ambitions down till you lose hope, there is strength in continuing for your passion.

"I am glad that you shared this with me" Shree gave him strength.

"Now I got it..." she said with deep thought.

"What?" Akash asked.

"That's why you don't like girls" and she laughed.

"Hahaha... not because of her. but my experience was very bad so I just don't trust anyone now" he tried to explain his point of view.

"Then why are you so polite with me? "She wants an answer.

"Because I know that you are a well-mannered girl," he answered.

"It means that you already know about me and my family," she looked at him.

"Maybe... you know, I am a magician" he answered with a smile.

"Ohh, right..."

Akash called her after getting free from the office and they went to Akash's house. His mother already knows about her and now they have family terms.

"He always used to talk about you and your progress in the office. I know that you are a hard-working girl" His mother compliments her.

"Thank you, aunt. Where is Uncle?" Shree asked about Akash's father.

"He is in the office" They start to discuss Akash and his childhood stories.

"He is my only son. I am very concerned about him and his future. I always wish to have a daughter like you."

"I am just like your daughter's aunt and Akash also protects me like a sister" She was praising his brother.

"I must say, he is very well-raised," Shree said with a smile.

After having dinner, Akash went to Shree's house to drop her off.

They were having a smooth life when all of a sudden Akash's mother kept on insisting on him getting married. She starts requesting him to choose a girl for him but he always refuses by giving illogical reasons.

But the fact was, he was scared of relationships. He doesn't want to believe or rely on anybody.

While arguing with Rahul, he said:

"I think all these emotions make a man very weak from inside. You become emotionally dependent on someone and I don't want to do that again. I am happy and I begged all of you to just let me live my life."

Akash is hurt again when her mother talks to Rahul to convince him to get married. He became upset again with everyone.

Akash still believes in Shree and he treats her like his own sister.

He called her once and discussed that he didn't want to get married.

"It's okay if you don't want to, I am with you and I will talk to your mother If you want me to do so"

"Yes please." He replied.

"Okay, don't worry. Now let's go for a coffee" Shree insisted on hanging out because she wanted to change his mood.

They went for an outing and then he dropped her home.

When he came back, his mother called him.

"Where were you?" she inquired in a serious tone.

"I was with Shree. We went to have coffee" he answered without looking at her.

"Are you angry with me?" she asked as she held her son's hand.

"Of course, not Mom... I just want you to understand that I don't want to get married yet" he explained.

"I got it. But you have to give me one solid reason to not get married" she asked.

"I want to live my life on my terms. I want to be free. I am afraid of any commitment"

It's normal to be afraid of the unknown. The unknown of what lies ahead after making a major decision can make us unsure of our future steps. However, for other people, uncertainty escalates to terror, and they may refuse to make any decisions at all. Akash was suffering from the same issue. Early experiences or even trauma may be linked to a fear of commitment or long-term relationship anxiety.

Akash was fearful of being abandoned, mistreated, or deceived if he committed suicide.

He spends the next few days alone, working day and night at his office. In the meantime, Shree discussed the whole situation with his mother and they decided not to disturb him again.

Shree called him at the weekend to make a plan but he didn't respond well so she decided to surprise him.

Akash's mother was reading a book in her room when her phone rang and she received the call.

"Hey aunt, can you do me a favor?" she asked.

"Sure, what do you want?" his mother replies.

"I need your help. I have a plan to surprise Akash as you know that he is not feeling good nowadays... so" she stopped here.

"Sure, what can I do for you?" his mother asked about the details of the surprise.

"Aunt, I want you to contact Rahul and some of his close friends, and invite them to your place. I will arrange a party there as I have taken a leave for tomorrow" she explained the whole plan.

"That's a great idea. How lucky Akash is, to have a friend like you" his mother was feeling proud of Shree.

"Thanks, aunt, I just want to make him happy. Please make sure that it's a secret between us" Shree sounded excited when Akash's mother agreed to help her in executing the plan.

The next day, she messaged Akash that she wouldn't be able to come to the office because of some health issue.

Everything went well that day, luckily.

Shree decorated the drawing room and made props for the evening. Akash's mother cooked his favorite food.

His mother called him to find out about his arrival.

"I am just a 15-minute drive away from home, Mom," he answered on the phone while driving.

"Okay..." his mother replies.

"But why are you asking Mom? Is everything all right?" he asked with curiosity.

"Yes, all is well. Just come home" she said looking at Shree who was smiling.

"Okay... but you are sounding suspicious to me," he asked again.

"Hahaha... no way. Okay, I am waiting... bye" and she disconnects the call.

After a few minutes, Akash opened the door and his eyes became teary when he saw all the preparations especially done for him.

He was overwhelmed with emotions when he hugged his mother. He was completely submerged by his thoughts and emotions about all of his life's current problems, to the point where he felt frozen.

He was unable to count the blessings of his life. Everyone had a very good time there and at night, he sent a heartfelt note in a text message to Shree, his parents, and friends.

A good laugh and a good long sleep are the two best cures of anything and that day, he had experienced both of these.

CHAPTER FOUR

'THE NEW TRIANGLE'

Shree was writing on paper when Akash knocked at her office door. She smiled.

"I know why you are here..." Shree starts the conversation. Akash sits on a chair and stares at her with a smart look.

"It is good to be smart, but you should at least pretend or act dumb sometimes for your loved ones," Akash said when he placed a small red-colored box on the table.

"WHAT?" Shree screamed.

"I know that I asked you to act dumb for my happiness or the sake of surprise but, not to overreact" he laughed while conveying his thoughts to Shree.

"No, I mean... what is this" she looked confused.

"You just said that you know my purpose for visiting your office today..." he replied.

"Yes, I said so... but I don't know about this. I thought you were here to thank me for the party I arranged for you yesterday,"

"Okay, pretty smart. But you are right" he said.

"Then why are you overreacting on this?" he added.

"Forget it. just tell me, what is it?" Shree asked with excitement.

"It's a gift..." he replied with a smile.

"Gift for?" She wants him to complete the sentence.

"Gift... I mean it's a thank-you gift for the party... yesterday" he tried his best to make her understand, but she was just confused.

"OH right... I know that you are here to Thank You. But I was not expecting this gift... that's why" she got emotional.

"Hahaha... you are a stupid girl..." he laughed at her stupid sister.

"That's what I know already..." She grabbed the small box from Akash and opened it. The box has a beautiful pair of ear studs in it.

"Beautiful.... It's beautiful, thank you Akash" she tried to control her emotions.

"Hey, stupid... don't cry. I want to say thank you for making so much effort for me. You always support me and cheer me up whenever I am down. This is just a small present from my side to say, "Thank you to the most genuine sister in the world." This time Akash got emotional.

"I have no idea that you can prepare a speech for me..." she places her hand on her mouth while laughing.

"I mean, this is so emotional..." she laughed again.

"Ha ha ha... very funny" Akash got offended. He stands up to leave the room when she holds his hand.

"Okay, okay, I am sorry Big-B, please sit..." she requested him to stay.

"I was kidding. I know how much you love me..." Shree looks serious this time.

They sat there for a few minutes, talking about their families, and then he went to his room to finish some tasks.

"Hey, Akash" someone knocks at his door. He looked there. It was his boss.

"Yes, sir... please come" he stands up from his chair to greet him.

"I know Akash that you are doing great. I have planned to give a new project to you." His boss has explained something to him.

"That's so kind of you. I am just trying to do my best in this office" he replied humbly.

"I have a group of people from another company, and you guys have to work on a joint project. I want you to lead on behalf of our company" His boss explained.

"Sure, sir... in fact, I am glad that you chose me for this" Akash said humbly.

"No, actually you deserve it," Boss replies.

After some more discussions about the project, his boss left the room and Akash called his mother. He asked about her schedule because he wanted to go with her for dinner.

"By the way, what was the reason behind this dinner?" his mother asked.

"I got a new project, actually a very good project and I want to celebrate it with my mom, so..." he explained.

"I am so proud of you my son..." his mother sounded proud of her son.

They had a quality time here, and then they left because Akash had to do some work for his new project. Shree didn't know about it yet.

The day in the office, Akash was in the meeting room when Shree messaged him. "Where are you?"

"In a meeting," he replied. Shree didn't reply because she knew he would contact her, once he was free. They work in the same office, but their floors are different. That's why Shree had to find him sometime.

His meeting went great and the boys were very passionate about their work. In this group of people, there was a guy named Ajay, but everybody called him AJ. He was one of the leading guys from another company.

While heading towards the gate, he noticed a girl discussing something very serious with one of her colleagues. AJ stopped for a moment. Shree looked at him and they made eye contact. It was a magical moment for AJ but Shree didn't notice.

Shree had a dusky complexion but she got a damn attractive face. She was beautiful and it was her sudden smile that caught AJ's attention.

He went off to his home but couldn't stop thinking about that girl. Due to his work ethic, he can't connect with her.

After a month, when he was free again to do his things, he called her.

"Sorry, may I know your purpose for calling me?" Shree answered his call, but she was hell confused.

"I will answer all your questions, face-to-face... I just want to meet you once. I don't want to disturb you, please don't get me wrong... I am a working person and recently I worked with XYZ company ...." AJ was trying his best to convince Shree of the meeting.

"OH right. So, you know me, right?" Shree first got shocked then she asked him a question.

"Not that much, but I want to know you..." he answered.

"I will let you know about my decision in a while" and she disconnected the call.

Shree was walking on her lawn, with a cup of coffee in her hands when she received his first call. That night, she kept thinking about him. Who is he? Why does he want to meet her? What happened after that? Should I tell Akash about all this?

She was in great confusion, but she was clear in at least one thing, that she would not inform Akash about this call. AJ requests her not to tell Akash about him.

"Time?" She typed this message and sent it to him, the next morning.

"After your office timing." He replied.

"Can I come to pick you up?" his second message was received.

"No," she replied with confidence.

"No problem. I am glad that you spare some time for me," he replied.

During their tea break, she told Akash that she had to go somewhere for some work so that he would not wait for her.

"Shopping?" he asked about the reason to go alone.

"No, I have to meet an old friend." She replied.

"Oh, okay..." Akash was unbothered so he didn't ask about her plan that much.

After their office time, she went straight to the restaurant he told her about. AJ was already there.

"So, I am here. Please tell me the purpose of this meeting. Shree said to him while looking into his eyes. He was looking nervous, or maybe he was a shy person. He was wearing a dark blue formal suit that suited him.

AJ was a tall, handsome, and good-looking guy.

"Amm, actually..." he was trying to talk.

"Why are you so nervous? And how do you know me?" She has plenty of questions to ask.

"I like you..." he said straight.

"What? Are you mad? Do we know each other?" she was about to throw a plate at him. His confession made her laugh.

"Hahaha... you are looking like a scared child and also an insane human being at a time... I am amazed..." Shree laughed at first. She was trying to know his intentions.

"I first saw you at your office..." then he told her a long story in short.

They ordered coffee and Shree spent some time in silence, trying to understand what he just said.

"I am not in any hurry, Shree..." he said while looking at the floor. He was shy.

"You can take your time, and I want you to consider all my confessions before making any decision," he added.

"Sure. I think I should go now" She grabbed her bag and left.

She was very confused about him until one day, her friend called her. She told her about his life story and how she lost someone she loved.

"We have no idea how much time we have left with our loved ones."

"I used to think a lot about life, I used to plan my life, though it's good... but now I believe to live in the moment" Her friend who just lost her love explained her tragic love story to Shree and she started relating her life with her friend.

Shree becomes emotional and she messages AJ that she has decided to give him a chance.

They met at the coffee shop.

"A chance?" AJ tried to digest her sentence. She only gave an approving smile.

"If you are not okay with my decision, then..." she looked at him as if she wanted him to decide right now.

"No... No, I am okay. I mean I agree" he replied at once.

"So, friends first?" Shree asked.

"But please remember that you have promised me not to tell Akash about all this until you become sure about our relationship" he requested.

"I know, and I better know how to keep my promises..." She sounds a little offended this time.

"Okay Thank you so much" he replied and took the last sip of coffee.

"Is it okay for you, if I ask you to go shopping with me?" AJ asked.

"Shopping, for?" Shree counters-questions him with surprise.

"Casually... I want to give you a gift" AJ replies.

Shree laughed.

"Gift for?" she again questions him.

"As a first gift, in the memory of this day... when we first meet" he blushed while replied to her question.

"Hahaha... it's cute. But I can't take anything from you..." She paused after saying this and continued "Maybe later" She stopped here.

"Okay, no problem," AJ agreed.

Shree was a sensible girl. She knows how to maintain a balance in her life, whether it's teamwork or her personal life. Balance and patience are the keys to success. She respects AJ but she is not in any hurry so she decides to give time to her relationship but doesn't want to confess in front of him.

She talked about all these scenarios with one of her friends and told her all about AJ. She listened to her with care but was not sure about him until she received a text message.

It was a long romantic text message that melted her heart.

"I will love you, cherish and adore you for as long as I live. This morning, I pray that God stays with you, guides your way, and blesses you in the way you least expect. If there is one thing I wish to see at all times, it will be to see that beautiful smile on your face. Have a day as wonderful as yours. I love you now, tomorrow, and forever. From AJ"

She received this message on the day after their meeting. Shree was planning to do some laundry when she received this beautiful confession and she couldn't stop herself and replied to him.

"I am honored. Dinner tonight?" She typed this and sent it to him.

"Am I dreaming? (With heart emojis)" AJ replies. He was pleasantly surprised.

"What do you think?" now Shree has decided to tease him properly.

They chat for a few minutes and then Shree finishes her home chores.

It was the first time; she was excited to meet him. She planned a proper date tonight.

"I am waiting outside..." AJ texted her.

"Coming..." she replied within a minute.

She was standing in front of a mirror in blue attire. She looked dazzling and super cute. She did her makeup and used a lot of highlighters on her cheeks and collarbone. She straightened her long hair and covered the front one from the top of the head in a fancy pin.

Her sincerity and purity are reflected in her eyes, and that is her unique characteristic. It was 8 PM when she stepped out of her house.

AJ had seen her in a casual dress before, but he never imagined her like that. He was surely going sane for her. She was thinking of his first reaction and smiling, with butterflies in her stomach.

She told her mom that she was going to a formal gathering. AJ opened the door for her as she stepped out of her house.

"Thank you..." Shree said when she sat in the front seat. He was completely impressed.

"Thank you for making my day. You are looking beautiful" he compliments her first because only a few men know that women love to be praised. He wants to pass this trial period at any cost.

They reached their destination after half an hour. It was a well-known restaurant with dim lighting. They choose to sit at a corner table.

"Can I hold your hand?" AJ managed to ask.

"Sure," and she offers her hand to him. Her nails were neatly shaped and covered with black nail paint.

He praised her beauty and talked about their favorite things and hobbies.

"So, what do you like to have for dinner?" he asked.

"I think we should order first so that we can chit-chat with each other..." AJ added.

"Sure..." Shree, a confident and independent girl, was feeling shy for the very first time in her life. AJ orders the food.

"Your hands are soft, by the way..." AJ compliments her again.

She tried to hide her smile. After some time, the waiter served their order.

"I think you like desi food the most..." AJ asked.

"Yes, and what do you like the most?" She asked this time.

"You..." he tried to stop his smile. Shree laughed at once.

"I know it's a bit cheesy, but it's true..." AJ defends himself.

Hours pass by and they get so involved in each other with every moment. Hands in hands, staring at each other, giggling, and enjoying the presence of their perfect date partners with each other, they were looking adorable.

"Tell me more about your family?" AJ asked.

"Are you sure you want to know all this right now?" Shree was just checking his level of commitment towards her.

"Of course, I am very serious about you..." he answered. Shree took a sigh of relief. They discussed their families, their hobbies, and their favorites honestly.

Every relationship is different, and people meet for a variety of reasons. Sharing a similar objective for what you want your relationship to be and where you want it to go is part of what characterizes a healthy relationship. And you'll only know that if you have a long and honest conversation with your partner.

Life was feeling like a fairytale to both of them. But unfortunately, it is not so easy to pass.

They finished the dinner and went to the car. AJ again opened the door for her and she got in. They were going home; AJ took a long route so that they could enjoy the company of each other.

"I want to say something..." Shree looked serious this time.

"Please go ahead..." AJ was holding her hand when he answered. Her hand was in his grip.

"Do you think that there is a difference between falling in love and staying in love?" Her face was straight towards the front mirror when she spoke her heart out.

"I know it's very easy for you to be in this relationship, or maybe you liked me, but…" she said something when AJ held his grip on her hand and she felt the warmth of his heart with his hand.

"Relationships require ongoing attention and commitment for love to flourish…" she continued.

"And…" she was about to complete the sentence when AJ turned his face toward her and stopped the car.

"Why are you so scared of commitment?" He asked her a question straight forward because he wanted to know all her fears.

"I am not scared of commitment, it's just that… all this is very new to me" she replied. Her heart was beating very fast.

"I love you, and I mean it…" AJ said in one go. Shree was very scared before that, but his words gave her the strength to smile. Her heart skips a beat when he confesses his love for the very first time in front of her. He was holding her hand in a car on a long wide road at night. It was like a dream come true situation for her.

Most couples find that their early dating days of face-to-face communication are increasingly being replaced by hasty texts, emails, and instant messages.

While digital communication is useful for some things, it does not have the same positive influence on your brain and nervous system as face-to-face communication. It was the face-to-face conversation that made Shree so relaxed at once and she realized that can trusted this man.

"So, you are just leaving…" AJ said with cute and sad expressions. Shree loved his innocent face so she gave him an affectionate smile.

They looked happier and calmer than ever, as they were unaware of the future. Of course, no one knows what fate has in store for them!!

'GROWTH IS A PROCESS'

"Hey... are you there?" Shree was typing an email on her laptop when her phone notification tone caught her attention.

"Yes. Why are you still up?" she replied. It was 2 AM and she was working on a project which is why she was still awake.

Akash sends a laughing emoji to her.

"Have you gone crazy?" she replied.

"What is the meaning of "C.R.A.Z.Y" in your dictionary?" Shree received this message as an answer. She thought that he might be disturbed so she called him.

"Now, tell me... what's the problem?" Shree asked on the phone call.

"Nothing... I was..." Before he completes his sentence, Shree interrupts him.

"I want to know the actual reason... no excuses" Shree orders.

"I am disturbed... I want to sleep, but I think I need to calm down first" He tried to explain.

"What happened? What are you thinking?" she asked again. She shuts down her laptop because she wants to listen to her Big B.

"Just thinking about all these relationships and... all the" he stopped suddenly. Shree felt that his voice was shaking.

"Hey bro, go on ... I am listening" Shree tried to give him the strength to speak.

Sometimes we are so tired of holding on to things that are making us weak, that one day... we just quit or we want to quit badly. Akash after his breakup with Anshu tried his best to forget about her or what she did to him, but unfortunately, after so many years, he was in the same pain. The pain of being betrayed, being left alone, being treated wrong, and being ignored! These are the worst things ever. You can relate this to physical pain. Physical injury and pain can be healed in a period, but the wounds on your soul can never leave you alone.

They kept on knocking on the door of your heart, after a specific period. Akash was going through the same when he was talking to Shree.

"I am starting to get worried that I won't be able to keep up the facade much longer and that the real I will emerge. And I wish I could figure out what was wrong. Maybe it's something to do with how foolish my entire life has been. I'm not sure. Why does the rest of the world put up with the hypocrisy, they need to put a happy face on a sad situation, and the urge to keep going?" he explained with a heavy voice.

"Is it related to your past...?" Shree asked a simple question that was not simple for Akash.

"I don't know... It's just that I am feeling disturbed as if something is missing in my life" he answered.

"That's why Aunt advised you to think about getting married this year" She tried to make him laugh but he became offended and disconnected the call.

Shree calls him back many times but he doesn't pick up. She was concerned about him so he sent him a message. "Text me as soon as possible or at least inform me about your condition"

"I am fine" She received this message the next morning; Akash sent him late at night. She decided to meet him in the office so she went there after placing all his belongings at her table. To her shock, Akash was not there.

She inquired about him from the office and they told her that he was late today.

Around noon, he arrived at the office. He was looking disturbed so Shree did not disturb him. After their office timing, she called him.

"Can you drop me home today?" she asked.

"Sure, I am waiting in the car," he answered.

She stepped into the car but didn't speak a word.

"I am sorry for the previous night. I was disturbed..." Akash starts the conversation with this confession.

"I think you need a change..." Shree gave him a bit of sincere advice.

"Change?" Akash asked.

"Yes, I have told Mom that Akash wants to meet you... she invites you for dinner tonight, with Uncle and Aunt," Shree said while searching for something on her phone from her bag. After a few seconds, she dialed a number.

"Hey aunt, how are you?" She said while her eyes were on Akash.

"Great. Is uncle there?" She was speaking to Akash's mother on the phone and then she invited his parents on behalf of her mother to her house.

"Okay, Uncle, see you tonight" She disconnects the call here.

"So, how do you want to give me a "change"?" Akash asked.

"It's just a family get-together and family is everything," Shree replies.

Akash dropped her home and went to his house. His parents asked him about the dinner and they all got ready in a short time.

"Why has she invited all of us today??" Akash's father said while driving the car.

"I don't know... "Akash replied.

"Akash... I have a feeling that you have been disturbed for some days. What's the matter, son?" Akash's father asked.

"Nothing Dad, just workload" Akash replies.

"Ahhh! There is nothing to worry about the workload. Life is full of challenges and one must know how to counter them. You are my brave son, you can do so many big things, you can do anything, son. All you need is to stay determined and concentrate on your career", his father advised him while they were heading toward Shree's place.

"Oh! Come on, dad. I know this but I am just a bit tired", he was frustrated and replied annoyingly.

When they reached there, Akash helped Shree in serving food to the other family members. After getting free from dinner, they all sit in the drawing room. Shree's mother was preparing tea.

"Uncle, I want to tell you something," Shree said while giving a mischievous smile to Akash. She continued.

"About Akash..." she added. Akash looked confused.

She was about to continue further when Akash interrupted her.

"Dad! Let me tell you first about today", he said

"No way, I am the one to tell you first", she argued.

Akash didn't listen to her and started speaking straightforwardly.

"Our boss scolded her today, very badly... and I think that incident has affected her brain cells" Akash counter-attacked. Everybody in the room started laughing.

"I think I missed something very interesting..." Shree's mother entered the room with teacups when she saw everyone giggling.

"Nothing special Mom," Shree answers. It was the first time today that Akash laughed. He realized this when everyone was busy having tea.

"Shree?" Akash proceeds to call her by name.

"What do you think, why does he sound disturbed?" his mother completes his sentences.

"We have some workload these days, so..." Shree decides to defend his brother this time when she notices his serious behavior again.

"Is it just me, or you guys also noticed that Akash was a little disturbed?" Shree's mother asked her after the guests left.

"Yes, mom... I will talk to him" Shree didn't answer properly.

When Akash reached home, he called Shree.

"What are you doing?" he asked.

"I was just doing the dishes. You reached home?" she asked.

"Yes, five minutes ago" he replied.

"Why did you arrange this dinner?" he asked.

"What type of a question is this? Of course, for you guys..." she answered.

"Why did you always do so much for me? I am already very thankful..." Shree interrupted him when he said this.

"Oo... hallo... I didn't do this to hear all these stupid things from you" she continued.

"Just tell me, how are you feeling now?" she asked about his mental state.

"I am trying to be better..." he answered.

"Great. Then do one thing more" She was in a mood to tease him again.

"Try to sleep early. Now go to bed otherwise you will be late for the office again" she replied.

"Hahaha..." he only managed to laugh at her purity. Shree disconnects the call.

"Good night, idiot" She received a text from his Big-B before sleeping. She places the phone on the side table and turns off the lights to sleep.

The next day in office, Shree became shocked when she came to know about Akash's resignation.

"Why?" She sends this message to Akash from her office.

"How's the surprise?" he replied.

"I will never talk to you again. You didn't even tell me about this. Bye," she typed this message with tears in her eyes and sent it to Akash.

"See you soon..." he replied but Shree was not interested in talking to him, at least after knowing that he left his job.

Everyone asked him but he didn't give any satisfactory reply to anyone.

"I just want to change my routine" He was trying to convince his parents, sitting in his drawing-room.

"I need a break Dad... and I hope that you will support me in this decision, as you always did for me" he was using an emotional blackmailing method to convince his parents here.

"Okay... enough for the day" Akash's father stands up from his chair.

"Akash, I am with you..." he always supports him in every decision of his life. He never fails to impress him by showing immense love and support to him. His mother kisses his forehead. No doubt he was a lucky child but the favorite one has to go through the toughest of trials.

Despite having all the blessings and luxuries of life, Akash sometimes feels that he is being tested by God. But why?

He was unable to find the answer but a wise man knows that God wants to know what's on our minds. He doesn't put us to the test to punish us. His tests are very similar to the ones we use in human interactions. We are testing the relationship when we invite someone to a party, join a club, play on a team, see a movie, go on a date, or spend the rest of our lives together in marriage.

Our next step of advancement, or, in certain situations, the conclusion of our search, is determined by whether we said "yes" or "no." Testing is how we figure out where we stand with someone we're trying to form a relationship with. It's the only way we can truly understand what "Trusting God" entails. When our faith is put to the test, it also puts our lives to the test.

Akash started to spend his time alone. He often felt that there was a void in his life. He wanted to move on, but couldn't do so.

Growth is indeed a process and every process takes time. The only thing that differentiates him from others is that he is in a continuous struggle.

One day, he was walking on the roof when he saw his mother coming towards him with his phone in her hand.

"Rahul wants to talk to you..." she gave him the phone.

"Hello?" Akash utters a word after a couple of days.

"Are you okay?" Rahul asked.

"Mmmm..." Akash didn't speak.

"I am coming back from my trip; I am coming to see you..." Rahul told him about his arrival. He was on a family trip that's why he doesn't know about his condition.

The next day, Rahul came to his place to see him.

"What have you done to yourself...?" Rahul looked worried for him.

"I am all right," Akash replies. They were sitting in his room, with their favorite cup of coffee in their hands.

"Aunt told me that you need a break... that's not a break! Stop being unreasonable Akash...this is not you" Rahul looked at him with pity. Akash was sitting idle.

"You are not a loser and stop behaving like one... I want you to fight. Fight and face every circumstance..." Rahul's words were affecting him. His facial expressions were changing every second.

"Shut up... just shut up" Akash finally spoke.

Losing his temper was an old habit of Akash. And Rahul was the one who knew how to tackle Akash during such a situation. Even though Akash's parents relied on Rahul because they knew that Rahul had the guts only to bring him back to his normal mood.

"Don't you dare try to act like my boss..." Akash throws a cup of coffee. Rahul stands up and tries to hug him but he pushes him away.

Akash was overrated but Rahul didn't even say a word. He wanted him to speak to him.

"Just go away, I can't fight anymore... I am tired... and if you don't want to see me like this, you can go... just go" Akash shouted at him. Also, he was trying hard to control his tears.

(Rahul was waiting for Akash to stop yelling at him)

"Hmm, hmm... It's okay... I am listening" Rahul again steps forward to him and hugs him tightly. Akash burst into tears.

"I can't fight. I can't fight anymore... I want to stay quiet. Forever..." Akash cried like a baby in Rahul's arms. He was slipping from his grip. They were on the floor after a few seconds.

Akash was in his lap. "I am tired..." Akash whispered.

"You can cry. I am there for you, and you know that" Rahul consoled him.

Akash needs a friend and Rahul is the only one who can handle him, that's why Akash's mother called him. He stays with Akash for a few days and convinces him to do some work.

"I am trying for a job, for you..." one day Rahul told him about his plan.

"So, that's why you are here?" Akash looks upset.

"Look Rahul, I don't want to join any office right now... I am not into any work" Akash tried to explain his issue.

"Okay, let's make it easy for you. If you don't feel like working there, you can resign. But please at least give it a try. It's an interesting job" Rahul spends some more time convincing him for the job.

Akash wasn't serious about his work, especially the time when he felt himself in the recollection of the past. He had lost his faith in his life. He didn't want to do anything. He was so disturbed that at a very young age, he didn't even have goals to achieve. It was a completely devastating moment when he lost his interest in life.

Apart from everything, it was the need of an hour to force Akash to work. The more time a man gives to his work, the more productive he becomes. Forcing him to do work was needed at that moment because his wounds were yet not healed. That's why Rahul didn't want him to go crazy just because of a single break-up of an immature love.

Long story short, after an argument of a couple of hours, Akash agreed. Everyone was happy. Rahul called Shree and broke the good news.

"Thank you so much, Rahul. You always helped him..." Shree was genuinely thankful to Rahul because she also tried her best to bring him back to life but this time, Rahul won.

"He is my brother... don't worry. He will be fine" Rahul replies.

After a few days, Akash joined his new office. It was a 40-minute drive away from his house.

"It's good to see you here, Akash. Rahul told me about you and your brilliant performances" His boss praised him on the very first day. It boosted his confidence.

He always thinks that he is blessed in every way, but that space in his heart makes him feel unlucky every time. Anyway, he decided to put some effort into this new job as he promised Rahul to never give up.

"You are my champion and I want to see you smile..." Rahul sent him this text message.

It was his first day so he didn't get any time for the phone. After his office time, he called Rahul first and told him about his day. He went back home, where Shree was already waiting for him.

"You can call me, or I mean, inform me at least..." Akash seems confused and a little embarrassed because he hasn't received her calls for a few weeks. She was very angry with him, but still, she managed to spare some time for him and came to meet him.

"I would love to inform you... if you receive my calls" Shree gave a cold reply.

"I am sorry... please?" Akash finally asked for the acceptance of his heartiest apology.

"It's okay..." she smiled and spoke. They have their dinner together and then Akash drops her home.

The next morning, Akash called Shree from his office.

"How are you... and AJ?" Akash asked.

"Oh, so you remember us?" Shree taunted him.

"So, it seems like my apology is still not accepted," Akash answers.

"Accepted. But this is the last warning" Shree said.

"So, what are your plans today?" Akash asked.

"Nothing special. Just routine work. What about you?" she answered.

"I am thinking of going outside today, I have asked Rahul about his schedule. If he responds on time, we will dine together, and you have to join us?" Akash narrates his plan.

"Me, you and Rahul?" Shree wants to confirm.

"Yes. Any problem?" Akash asked.

"No, not at all... anything for you," Shree answers.

"Great. I will update you in a while" Akash said and disconnected the call. Shree starts doing her work.

After talking to Shree, Akash's colleague enters his room.

"Boss has called an urgent meeting. We are waiting for you. I am here to inform you, please come" his colleague said in a hurry and left the room.

Akash stood up in a minute and went towards the meeting room. He left his phone on his table. There was an emergency in their office. One of his colleagues had made a major mistake in a project, and the company was on the deadline. His boss called the meeting and asked everyone if anyone could do it again in a short period, voluntarily.

"I can do it, sir" Akash raised his hand and spoke.

"Are you sure?" his boss asked again.

"Yes, sir. I can do it before the deadline ends" Akash replies. Everyone looked at him with astonishment in their eyes.

"You are a newcomer, Akash; how can I trust you?" his boss said.

"Sir, I don't think so, you have any other option. Please let me handle this..." Akash looked confident when he said this to his boss.

"Okay, I am waiting. You have to work here, in the meeting room." His boss orders.

"Everyone please leave" his boss looked at his staff and spoke.

It was 1 PM when Akash started working. He was working with confidence. His boss was impressed already.

Akash forgot about their plan because he was so eager to work on this project that he didn't even realize that his cell phone was not in the room. Rahul and Shree called him many times but all in vain.

At last, at 9 PM Rahul comes to his office. He saw Akash working in the meeting room, passionately discussing the project with his boss. He didn't disturb him. He called Shree and informed him about the situation because she was worried too.

At 11 PM, he finished his task, and stepped out of the meeting room with his boss, with a bright smile on his face. He saw Rahul waiting outside for him.

"Oh, what are you doing here?" Akash asked shockingly.

"You better know. Where is your cell phone?" Rahul was in a bad mood. He wants to kick Akash in the face but can't do so because it is his office.

"I am so sorry, I forgot," Akash explained.

"I was stuck..." Akash said this when Rahul interrupted him.

"I know. The office boy told me about your schedule. But you can at least send us a message" Rahul said.

"Oh, Shree? I have to call her..." Akash rushes towards his room, but Rahul stops him

"I have already informed her. Now pick up your things, and come with me." Rahul orders.

"Oh, thank you..." Akash took a sigh of relief.

"Where are we going?" Akash asked Rahul. They were sitting in his car and Rahul was driving.

"On dinner" Rahul replies.

"Oh right," Akash said.

Akash was very happy today. He has completed challenging work in a very short time. He was continuously thinking that a man should never underestimate his potential. You never know how capable you are, until you do challenging work. To his surprise, he never knows that he can meet deadlines. It was a pleasant day for him. He was moving towards healing and positivity. But he was also worried about his friends whom he loved so much. He was thinking about Shree, and how to make her happy.

They reached the restaurant and were moving towards a table when Akash noticed that Shree was already there.

"You know about the plan. Rahul informed you?" Akash came close to her and asked these questions but she didn't reply. At that time, three of them were sitting at a table.

"Are you still angry with me? I was busy. Rahul, please tell her..." Akash looked at Rahul and asked for help.

(Rahul shrugged)

"I am out of it. You have to handle her on your own" Rahul replies. He starts looking here and there.

"Shree, let me explain... my boss" Akash turned his chair towards her and was about to say something when Shree looked at him and started laughing.

"You are a fool and stupid person," Shree said while laughing.

"I was very angry with you but I can understand that you were busy. But this is the last time... I will kill you next time if you repeat this" Shree continued.

"Thank God... I was so scared" Akash smiles.

Shree and Rahul could see clearly that their friend Akash was coming back to his life. He was getting responsible professionally. They both were so happy to see such an amazing change in Akash's life. All of them looked so satisfied. Shree and Rahul were satisfied because they found that they made it and their friend was back to life. On the other hand, Akash was super satisfied with his performance at the new place not to mention, he was super satisfied because of Rahul and Shree.

At that point in his life, while sitting at the tip of a restaurant with the two most sincere persons of his life, he again realized how blessed he was.

Every moment spent with them was priceless for him. Even when we look back on the struggles that we have faced, we can see how they ultimately made us stronger or taught us valuable lessons. These difficulties turned out to be blessings in disguise.

"Hey, what are you thinking?" Shree makes him aware that he is in a restaurant.

"I think we should order now," Rahul said.

"Yes, sure," Akash said with a smile.

He looked at both of them and a wave of inner happiness created a ripple effect in his heart. While sitting on a rooftop, he looked at the sky and smiled. Time flies!

CHAPTER SIX

'THE MYSTERY'

In the joy of their recent success (completion of the project) Akash's boss announces a party on the coming weekend. Everybody linked to his company was invited to this party. Akash was the one who was in the light and everybody was praising him.

His boss looked happy as their company got a lot of profit from this project. "At first, I decided to throw a party on this occasion but now, after seeing the passion of my dedicated and hardworking employees, I am announcing a one-month bonus for the whole staff" his boss announced.

Everybody becomes happy with the announcement. People want to meet Akash as he is the person of the night.

"Hey Akash, I want to congratulate you on your success. And thank you very much, on behalf of our whole department as we got a bonus just because of you." one of his colleagues said.

"That's very kind of you, "Akash said looking at him. There was a group of people standing behind him.

"Let me introduce you to the main team of my department..." the new boy pointed his hand toward the people standing on one side.

"Ishaan, Amar, Suhani, Ananya, Jaya, Advik, Aarush, Dipankar and myself Ayaan" the new boys introduced his team.

"Hello everyone…, Akash" Akash looked at them for a second and introduced himself.

"Thank you so much for your time, sir," Ayaan said.

Then everyone moves towards the dinner table and the party goes on. Akash was sitting on the front table with a glass of cold drink in one hand, looking at others.

Why are they looking so happy today?

Looking?

Are they genuinely happy or just looking happy?

Akash used to judge every person. He was looking at the crowd while thinking about them when someone hit him on the back of his head. He turned around and was amazed to see one of his classmates at this party.

Karan was his class fellow, and Akash recognized him at once.

"Hey… I just came to know about your achievement," Karan said.

"Karan? Long time man… what are you doing here?" Akash said with excitement.

"My wife and I were invited to a birthday party on the second floor of this complex. I saw a banner outside this hall with your name, so I asked someone about you, and here I am" Karan explained.

"Great. I thought you were the hidden part of our company" Akash said with laughter.

"No, no," Karan replies.

"Come with me. I will introduce you to my wife," Karan insisted Akash come with him.

"Sure," Akash said and started walking behind him.

"Anshu is a very sweet person. We had an arranged marriage" Karan said and Akash felt that someone hit his head so hard that his body trembled while stepping down from the stairs.

"Are you all right?" Karan asked and held his hand.

"Yes... I am all right" Akash tried to smile.

At that very moment, a girl appeared in front of them and looked at Karan.

"I was looking for you. Where have you lost?" the girl said.

"Akash, meet my wife Anshu. Anshu, he is Akash, my class-fellow. We are just coming to you. I want to introduce you to him" Karan explained.

"Hello," Anshu looked at him and smiled. Akash breathes easily when he finds out that she is not his Anshu. It was another girl. They stand there for a few minutes and then the newly wedded couple leaves.

Akash first laughed at himself and then he felt pity for him.

Why is life a strange place to live? Why is it so unpredictable? Why can't we control our life? After all, it's our life!

These questions were making him crazy when he was sitting in his room. He went straight to his mother and hugged her.

"Why didn't you tell me that your temperature is high?" Akash's mother said to him. She tried to show her deep concern to him.

"Mom??? Stop taunting..." Akash looks offended when his mother teases him because he hugged her after a long time.

She laughed.

He spent a good quality time with his mom and dad that night. They talked about his childhood. His parents were surprised to see this change but they were happy because it was a pleasant change.

"I think he has become mature now..." his father said to his mother when Akash left their room.

He went to his room to sleep but sat on a chair. Take a deep breath and try to smile. He was happy that he had finally controlled himself. Maybe he has learned to forget about her!

The next day in his office, he met Rahul.

"Hey, are you free for some time?" he received his text message.

"Yes," Akash replies.

After fifteen minutes, Rahul knocks at his door. "I hope that I didn't disturb you..." Rahul said when he stepped into his office.

"Not at all. Please come" Akash stands up to greet him.

"I have to meet a client nearby, but unfortunately, he is late. So, I thought why not your office" Rahul said.

"Great. Tea or coffee?" Akash asked. "Coffee" Rahul replied and Akash ordered the same for him.

"So, what's up? How's everyone treating you after a big achievement? Are you enjoying this fame?" Rahul asked with a long wide smile.

"I met Karan yesterday," Akash said. Rahul could sense that Akash was trying his best to control a burst of laughter.

"Karan? Our class fellow?" Rahul asked.

"Yes," Akash replies.

"Then what's so funny in it? Why are you behaving like that?" Rahul asked.

"Because his wife's name was Anshu" Akash laughed. Rahul saw the pain in his eyes.

"Not that Anshu. I mean she was not my Anshu..." Akash continued.

"She was some other girl. I have met her too. such a cute couple. You know what's funny?" Akash explained yesterday's incident and Rahul listened quietly.

"I thought she was my Anshu..." Akash told him the whole incident. Rahul feels that he is behaving abnormally. He should have been sad, but he was laughing and it disturbed Rahul.

"You are looking like an idiot" Rahul looked at his eyes and spoke.

"You think I am joking?" Akash asked. Meanwhile, the office boy served them coffee.

"I thought we discussed us... and planned something, but I think you need time," Rahul said when a boy knocked at the door.

"May I come in sir?" the boy asked. Akash nodded.

"Sir, the boss wants to see you in the meeting room at 10 AM," the boy said and left. It was 9 AM at that moment.

"Rahul, you are getting me wrong. I want to share this with you, just to make you believe that I completely get over her. I am fine. Look at me... am I looking sad to you?" Akash said while looking at his eyes. It was the first time when Rahul noticed that he was not lying.

"If it's true then I am more than happy for you" Rahul replies. Rahul's phone rang and he checked his phone. It was his client's call and was calling him at the meeting place.

"I will call you tonight," Rahul said and left his office. While walking towards the exit gate, he saw a girl entering the lift. He thinks that it's Suhani but he was in a hurry so he didn't approach her.

At night, Akash's phone rang.

"Hello," he received the call. Rahul was on the line.

"Hey, Akash. How was the day?" Rahul asked.

"As usual. I attended a meeting with the teams of some other departments of my office, right after you left the office, and then I had lunch with Shree..." Akash suddenly stops while informing him about his routine.

"But why are you asking about my routine?" Akash asked.

"Do you have any girl named Suhani in your office?" Rahul asked a question again.

"I don't know... I mean how can I remember the names of every employee" Akash replies.

"Oh yeah, right..." Rahul said.

"Why are you asking dude?" Akash questions this time.

"Nothing special. I just saw a girl in your office, I mean on the ground floor of that building, and I think I know her, but I was in a hurry so..." Rahul explained his issue.

"Hahaha... then what's so stressing in it?" Akash said.

"Hahaha... It's not stressing, I just want to confirm..." Rahul also laughed at his stupidity. The two best friends then talk for a few minutes more and the call disconnects.

The next day, Akash came to know about a new project and he had to work on it with some new members and some volunteers from other departments. Everyone introduced himself/herself and there, Akash met Suhani.

He suddenly remembers that maybe Rahul was talking about her. After the meeting, everyone leaves. The new members shifted to this floor so he went to her during the tea break.

"Hey... Suhani?" Akash said hesitatingly.

"Yes... and you Akash?" Suhani recognized him.

"We met at the office success party. Ayaan introduced us. I think you don't remember, but I know you..." Suhani said with a smile.

"Oh Right. Do you know Rahul?" Akash asked.

"Rahul Roy?" she asked with shock.

"Yes..." Akash replied with a smile.

"Do you know him?" Suhani looked curious.

"He is my best friend" he gave her a wide-mouth smile.

"Oh great. I did not know that he worked here. How do you know about me?" Suhani looks excited.

"He used to visit me quite often. he saw you here, a couple of days ago... and he asked me but I didn't know your name" and they both started laughing.

Akash told him the whole story and they enjoyed their tea with gossip about Rahul and Suhani.

"We used to play with each other. We spent a part of our childhood together, but my family had to shift to America and we moved there..." Suhani talked about his relationship with Rahul.

"His mother is a very good friend of my mom. So, you can say that we have good family terms..." Suhani continued.

"It's good to have you here" Suhani smiled.

"Same here... see you in the meeting" Akash replies. They both end their first meeting here, unaware of what has already been written in their fate.

"Hey, you were right. Suhani works here" Akash sends this message to Rahul.

They attend the final meeting regarding their new project and Suhani volunteers in Akash's team. They start working on it. Shree was also very busy these days so Akash didn't get a chance to introduce Suhani to Shree. Although they work for the same company, their department and nature of work were different.

The transitional phase had been starting for Akash. He didn't notice it but could easily feel the difference between this Akash and the old Akash. He was a boy who never liked to work, a boy who didn't want to work in an office but now he had become a workaholic. Now work was everything to him.

Akash was trying his best to enjoy his busy schedule. He was become the kind of man who can never sit idle. He healed himself to some extent and that was the reason for the best performance in his work.

After a week, Rahul visited Akash's office but he was in a meeting. He was waiting for him when he stepped into the office with Suhani and other teammates discussing something.

"Oh, Rahul...I am sorry, I was in a meeting" Akash said when he saw him sitting in his office.

"It's okay. I am here to pick you up for a lunch plan" Rahul said.

"Okay, just give me 10 minutes" Akash replies.

"Everybody please settle down..." Akash said to his teammates. He explained some important points to them and ended the meeting.

"Suhani, you please stay there..." Akash said to Suhani and she understands that Akash doesn't want to reveal his earlier interaction with her in front of his colleagues.

"It's good to see you here" Rahul starts the conversation.

"Same to you. Akash told me about your friendship" Suhani replies.

"What about going on lunch together? We can easily talk here" Akash suggested a plan. Both of them agreed.

"Great. Let me ask Shree about her availability" Akash continued.

"Oh, I forgot to talk about Shree. She is my sister and she works here" Akash said to Suhani. Shree was also available for lunch but she said that she would join in half an hour. So, the three of them went to a restaurant.

"Please order my favorite steak, otherwise I will kill you... I am just coming" Shree messaged Akash. He laughed at once and both of them noticed.

"Girlfriend?" Suhani asked from Akash. Rahul looked at her as if she had made a mistake but to Rahul's surprise, Akash just smiled. He told her that it was Shree on the chat.

After a few minutes, Shree appears. She was shocked to see a girl at Akash's table.

"Hey everyone," Shree said and sat on a chair.

"Shree, she is Suhani. Our colleague and Rahul's family friend" Akash introduced them.

"Great. Nice to meet you... so you work in our office?" Shree asked.

"Yes, actually I am from a different department but recently I volunteered on a project so I had a chance to work with him" Suhani answered.

"Right..." Shree replied but she was still confused. A girl, with Akash! Hard to imagine, and she was seeing it with open eyes.

"I don't want to talk about AJ to anyone yet. Till we decide to make it official" Shree sent this message to Akash while sitting there.

"Don't worry. Focus on your favourite food" he replied with a lot of laughed emojis.

They had a very good time. It was the start of their new journey, both in their professional and personal life. They were going to realize it soon.

After a few days, Suhani again got a chance to work with Akash as she gained experience in this field and her performance was brilliant. She was an intelligent and good-looking girl with straight brown hair. She was the kind of ideal heroine with a slender body. Rahul once told Akash, that boys were crazy for her in college times.

Suhani and Akash became good friends in a few weeks because they used to spend a lot of time together. They completed their next project too. Akash's parents also came to know about his new friend and his new success.

"We are proud of you my son," his father said to him for the first time in his professional career in front of everybody when they were having a family dinner with Shree and her mother at their house.

"I am glad that he is looking better and fresher than last time" Shree's mother continued.

"Now, we should think about his marriage," Shree's mother said to tease him. Everybody laughed, and Akash enjoyed it too.

One day at the office, Akash was informed that Suhani was absent due to illness. He thought he should ask about her health.

"Hey, how are you now? It's Akash here." He typed this message and sent it to Suhani. And then a series of never-ending discussions that convert into gossip start that day.

"I am fine, Thank You" She replied.

"How are you feeling now? What about your health?" he sends another text.

"It's just a viral infection. I will be back in a day or two." She replied with a smiling emoji this time.

"Right. Take proper rest and don't worry about the work" This time Akash also replied with a smile emoji.

"Thanks..." Suhani replies. Akash read this message and got back to work.

The next day, Suhani was absent again. He decides to call but due to his busy schedule and workload, he forgot to call her.

Also, Shree and AJ invite him to dinner. He had a good time with them and went back to his room late at night. So, he decides to send a message again. He didn't find it appropriate to call a girl at night, so he typed a message showing his concern for her health and sent it to her.

"Thank you. I am much better now. Don't worry" She replied within a minute. It was 12:15 AM.

"Patients should sleep early to take good care of their health..." Akash replied again.

"Hahaha... I was just about to sleep" Suhani replies. But their chatting session had started already.

They said good night to each other at 02:30 AM.

The next day Shree comes to his office. "Are you free?" she knocks at his door.

"Yes, please come in..." Akash nodded.

"I want to discuss something..." Shree said as she sat on a chair near him.

"Aunt is worried about you..." Shree continued.

"Oh god... mom called you again?" Akash becomes offended as he understands the matter in a second.

"Look Akash, I know that I am younger... but it doesn't mean," Shree said this when Akash held her hand.

"Shree, I just want some time... and I told her that I am not ready yet. Please don't force me. I promise I will not disappoint you" Akash almost begged her.

"Okay, but we want to hear a positive response soon," Shree said with a smile. Akash's mother often called Shree and asked her to convince him to marry but he always refused.

Suhani gets back to work after two days and they used to meet at tea-break daily.

After a month, she told him that she resigned from the job because she got a better opportunity due to her experience. Akash, Rahul, and Shree wish her good luck in the future. They decide to meet whenever they get the chance.

"How's your new job treating you?" Akash sends her this message when she comes back home after her first day at her new job.

"It's good... how are you?" Suhani replies.

"I am fine. Working on a project" Akash replied and then discussed their routine.

They used to talk almost daily but Rahul and Shree were unaware of this new friendship.

"Can I call you?" He received this message from Suhani one day.

"Of course," he replied. She called after a minute.

"Actually, sorry to disturb you at this time, I need a little help" Suhani sounds worried.

"Yes, please tell me what is it?" Akash answered. She explained one of her new ideas to him and asked about the suggestion.

"I want an expert to advise on this, so I thought why not you... I hope you don't mind" Suhani said on the phone call.

"Not at all" he replied. He explained the right method to her and helped her with the project. When she completed it, she offered him a treat.

"You have to come. It's on me. That way we get a chance to meet" Suhani insisted him.

"Okay, see you tonight" Akash agreed.

Suhani texted him the name of her favorite restaurant and Akash reached there.

He was entering the hall when Suhani noticed him and waved at him. She notices for the first that he is not an average-looking guy. She found him handsome at that moment but then he came close and said "Oh Hello..." and Suhani's fantasy world shattered in a second.

"Hey... how are you?" she answered.

"Where are you lost?" Akash asked.

"Nothing..." she took a minute to come back to reality then she continued.

"Long time..." she said with a smile.

"2 months actually..." she said again.

"Yeah right," Akash agreed.

They talked about their office and a new routine. Suhani told him about her new colleagues.

"Everybody is cooperative but not more than you," Suhani said. She was wearing a pink-colored long frock. Her beautifully styled hair makes her even more beautiful, but the man sitting in front of her shows zero interest in all this glamour. He didn't even notice her, but Suhani didn't mind because she was also not interested.

Their concern was to have a good time and to maintain a good working relationship. They ordered the food and Akash briefed him about some new strategies of work.

"I am very lucky to have you as my mentor, you always helped me a lot. Thank you for all the efforts you have made to date, and this treat is my way to say Thank you" Suhani said.

"Then I should eat like a horse because this is the last treat" Akash teased him.

"Hahaha... I didn't mean that" Suhani laughed.

The waiter asked for the bill and they left after that.

"Ice cream, from my side?" Akash asked when they were on their way home.

"Amm... Sure" Suhani agreed.

Suhani finds him a very gentleman. They spend a couple of hours together and Akash drops her home.

"Thank you for the yummy treat." Akash sent him a message when he lay on his bed after spending a wonderful day with Suhani.

"Pleasure is all mine" She replied.

Now, they used to chat every day without knowing what was written in their destiny.

'OBSTACLES ARE OPPORTUNITIES IN DISGUISE'

"What should I wear today", Akash asked himself because it was a special day for him.

"I should be more impressive than Suhani today", he said to himself.

"But first let me ask her, what is she wearing? Should I ask her or not? No, no, no, it would be so weird", he thought.

"Oh! come on Akash make up your mind", he asked himself.

Akash wants to wear something cool because he wants to look more perfect and more impressive than anyone at the party. It was Rahul's birthday, and Suhani was invited to his birthday as well.

"OK, Akash make up your mind. Let's go with the black shirt and black pants", he decided.

"Yes, it would be perfect", he finally made up his mind.

Akash used to do perfect things. He was a man who wanted the things around him completely spick and span that's why he takes so much time in choosing a dress. Although Akash is an average-looking boy, he has a very good personality. He got ready for the birthday party. Meanwhile, he was combing his hair, when Suhani called him.

"Hello! Akash, how are you? I just want to ask you if can you pick me up from my home because my car isn't working. I think it has some problem with its engine", she requested.

"Okay! Be ready. I'll be there around 8 PM", Akash replies.

He was a philogynist and he always respected women. Although, he had no sister he knew very well about the security issues a girl usually faces while driving alone.

That's why without further ado, he said that he is coming to her.

(It was already 7 O'clock)

He put on his watch not to mention his incredible wild scent. He was all ready to leave the house. When he was about to close the door of his room, suddenly he remembered that he had forgotten the gift, he bought for Rahul.

"Oh, the gift", he said.

He then opened the door of his room and grabbed the gift box from the cupboard.

"Now everything is ready. Let's go", he thought.

He sent a message to Suhani,

"I'm on the way to your home".

When he was about to leave for Rahul's birthday party, he heard the voices of harsh arguments between his father and his mother. He went downstairs and tried to calm them down. He asked them to stop this argument, but his parents were arguing so badly. They both were furious.

What's wrong with you guys? Why are you guys doing this?

"Ask your dad he is out of nowhere crying on me", her mother said.

"Just because of you Natasha! I lost my everything", his dad complained.

"What did you mean everything?", he asked.

"I lost everything, son, I lost everything Akash", his father cried.

His father faced a huge loss in his business.

Men don't appreciate a woman. They just blame the women most of the time. (Not all the men) Just like all other men out there, he was also blaming the woman for his loss.

His father had a huge investment in the business, but the utilization of assets and unproductive working capital management along with poor plans made him lose the project.

"I had invested my everything in that project", he said with a cry.

"It's okay Dad. Profit and loss are a part of the business", he tried to convince him.

"It's not okay. You will never understand this because you have no life experience", his father said.

This statement by his father made Akash so much disappointed. He didn't want them to argue anymore that's why he requested his mother to go back to her room and give some space to his father.

He asked his mother,

"Please go to your room. Don't you guys dare to argue again".

(He took her mother to the room and consoled her.)

"He is worried. Give him some space.

"He will be okay" he convinced her.

"But Akash, the loss?", she asked. (She had tears in her eyes)

"I'll handle it. Don't worry mother. I had saved that much enough to facilitate you guys from all the necessities", he said with confidence.

"Dad is not the only breadwinner of our family. I can earn and spend that money on my parents", he added.

She was feeling so proud of his son.

"Anyways Mom, It's Rahul's birthday. I have to go Mom", he told her. "I am leaving for Rahul's birthday. Okay? I'll be back soon. We will figure it out", he informed his mother.

"Yeah, I remember, you told me about your plan", she said. "Wait a minute, I got something for Rahul as well", her mother told him.

"Wow!", he was surprised.

(She went to the cupboard and grabbed a box from it)

"Here it is, take it. This is for my other son with a huge warm hug", she said.

Akash was inspired by the aura of his mother. He was more attached to his mother than his father.

Meanwhile, he was talking to her mother, when Suhani called him. He declined the call. She texted him,

"Where are you?"

(He read her message and left the house.)

Around 8:30 PM. He reached her home. He got out of the car and called her.

"Hello! I am at the gate. Come outside", he said.

He turned over his head, and he was astonished when he saw her amazing personality all dressed up to the nines. He has never seen her in such a getup.

She came closer to her and said,

"You look good, Akash".

Akash said with astonishment,

"I cannot believe that it's you. You look so amazing. I usually do not pay attention to others but your beauty forced me to tell you the truth."

"Thanks for your compliment, Akash. Let's go, we are already late", she said.

(He opened the door of the car for Suhani.)

"Wow, he opened the door for me", she thought to herself and sat in the car. She further thought, "Maybe it depends on the woman and the circumstances. For me, I appreciate the thoughtfulness and chivalry displayed by opening the door for me".

She was happy to see such nice behavior of Akash. She did not have any idea that Akash would be impressed this much by her. She thought that Akash was a career-centric boy and did not have an interest in girls because at that time Akash marginalized her as peripheral.

(They were heading towards Rahul's home)

In the car, Suhani asked Akash to play songs.

"Which song do you like? Hindi, English?", she asked.

"Of course, English songs because Hindi songs are not more than listening to puja pat or a gate to depression", he said and mocked.

"It isn't like that", she confronted.

"English songs are good but Hindi songs can help you to understand or feel the emotion", she gave the argument in her justification of Hindi songs.

"I don't think", he said.

"Ugh... But I am going to play a Hindi song right now", she said

"Ok, as you wish", he said.

She played the new song of the movie Ek Tha Tiger. She was enjoying the song but Akash was unconcerned. They both reached Rahul's place.

"Look at my beautiful friends", Rahul said.

"Hey, birthday boy, Happy birthday to you my brother, and here is your gift. Take it, and enjoy it", Akash said.

"Wow! But two gifts?", Rahul said.

"Yes, actually Mom bought it for you", Akash told him

"Aw... why didn't to bring her with you?", he asked.

"She was busy", Akash lied.

"Happy birthday, Rahul. It's a pleasure that you have invited me here", Suhani said.

(Not to mention, Rahul already knew Suhani from the high school. They were also family -friends)

"Thank you both of you. You guys look so beautiful. And trust me you both are looking incredible in black", Rahul said and he had a smirk on his face as well.

(Thank you they both said at the same time)

"Wait a minute? Where is Shree?", Akash asked.

"I called her. She didn't pick up my call", Rahul told him

"Let me call her", Akash said and brought his phone out of his pocket.

(Calling but not picking up)

"Are we going to celebrate your birthday without Shree?", Akash said

"We have to because everyone is waiting for the cake-cutting ceremony", Rahul said.

(Akash got upset for Shree, he was constantly calling her but she wasn't available. Suhani found it a little bit suspicious. She thought that maybe Akash was interested in Shree, and that's why he was worried for her. Lucky Shree, she got a good catch)

"Now come on let's cut the cake". I was just waiting for you guys. Trust me, let's go now", Rahul said

They all went to the hall to cut the cake. The party was not that much big, there were only some close friends of Rahul and Akash. Akash met many of his school friends as well. they enjoyed the whole party but Suhani was a stranger at that party. Rahul was trying to give her his attention but he was busy with his other male friends that's why he asked Akash to give her company.

"But I don't want to, Rahul", he said

"Please, go and accompany her. She is all alone Akash", Rahul insisted.

"Ugh... all right", he said and went to the Suhani.

"Hi, did you eat something?", Akash asked Suhani.

"Yeah, I am done with the food", Suhani replies.

"Ok. So do you know anyone here in Rahul's party", he asked.

"Yes, I know you and Rahul", she said.

"Anyone else", he said.

"Not really", she replied.

Akash was trying to talk to her but he was a bit reluctant to talk to the girls after his first separation from Anshu.

"Why did you come late by the way? Sorry, I forgot to ask this before. Was everything okay?", she asked.

"Yes, All good. It was just because of the traffic", he said. "I apologize for that", he said.

"I didn't you to apologize, I was worried for you", she said.

"Why were you worried for me", he replied.

"Because you are my workmate", she said.

"Ok, but I am good. There is nothing to worry about", he said.

"How is your job going?", he further asked

"It is going great", she said.

(A gap of silence)

"And what about your new job? You were telling me that you had qualified for a new job opportunity in Bangalore", she asked him.

"Yes, I have an interview there in the next coming week and I hope that I will ace it", he said confidently.

"I am sure, you will", she said.

They both talked a little bit more about careers and then Akash got a call from her mother. She was asking about his arrival because it was already late. He told her that he had to go now. He went to Rahul to inform him that he was about to leave.

"Hi, Rahul I have to leave. Mother is calling me. She needs me", he told him

"Is she okay?" Rahul asked with worry.

"Yes, she is fine. All good", he replied.

"Okay, sure. I'll visit her soon", he said.

"You are always welcome brother", Akash replies.

"And do not forget to thank her for the gift", Rahul reminded him.

Akash was about to leave Rahul's home but then he was called by Suhani.

"Wait Akash", she said.

"Yes Suhani", Akash replies,

"Can you do me a favour once again", she asked.

"Do you want me to drop you home?", he said.

"Pretty smart, and yes, I am sorry to bother you but I have no other option", she said.

"It's ok, come on. let's go then", Akash said.

Suhani said goodbye to Rahul and went back to the parking where Akash was waiting for her.

(Akash was once again calling Shree but she wasn't picking it up. Akash's concerns for Shree were making Suhani doubtful)

Akash played the song for Suhani before she asked for it.

"Why did you play it?", she asked.

"You were about to ask me for the song again, right?", he said

"I don't want to listen to songs at this time", she said

"What's wrong?", Akash asked. (Akash turned the song off).

"Because I don't want to", she said

(Suhani was having blues as she got insecure about the relationship between Akash and Suhani).

(They didn't talk to the home. They both wanted to talk but none of them was willing to take the initiative. He dropped Suhani at his home, and he didn't even wait for goodbye and went to his home.

When he reached home, his parents were asleep.

He went to his room straight. He laid down on the bed without changing his clothes.

He was about to fall asleep when his mobile started vibrating over and over. It was Rahul, sharing pictures of the birthday party in the WhatsApp group. Due to the vibration, Akash got up because it was annoying him. He grabbed his phone to put it on silent.

He was about to ask him about Shree but he saw one of Suhani's beautiful pictures. He usually used to surpass his intimation when he found anything attractive to him, but at that moment, he stared at her pictures with a shine on his eyes

"She is perfect", he unconsciously said.

He opened the folder to see other pictures. He saw one of his pictures with Suhani. It was a Candid picture since they were talking to each other. At the same moment, he got Rahul's message with a photo.

"Hmm... Not bad. You guys look great" (he was talking about Suhani's and Akash's candid photos).

"What a coincidence! I was looking at the same photo", Akash replied to him

Rahul sent him a heart emoji.

Meanwhile, Akash was checking other notifications, and he came to know that Suhani also texted him this,

"Thank you, Akash".

"There's nothing to thank, helping others is good", Akash replied her.

Luckily, she was up. She was thinking about Akash when he got his reply. She smiled when she got his message.

"Helping others is a good thing, I appreciate that", she replied to him

"You are up till late?", He replied

"I was about to sleep but your text message distracted me", she replied.

"I apologize for that. Good night", he replied.

"I was kidding", she said.

Akash didn't reply to her back.

(He forgets to call Shree and falls asleep)

(Akash was not an easy person to understand. He was a workaholic person. He was more professional than Suhani that's why it was easy for him to surpass the other emotions and to stay concentrated on his work)

"Dad?" He knocked at the door and addressed his father.

(The next day Akash went to his father's office to talk to him)

"Yes, my son", his father replies.

"How are you?" He asked his father.

"I am okay. I am sorry about the last day", he replied.

"Forget about that, I got you some coffee", he told his father.

"Oh, thank you", he said with pleasure.

"Dad! It's okay to have a materialistic loss in this world but the real regret one must have on losing their loved one is", he said to his father

"I can understand son but I can't help it. I spent my whole life investing in this company. I was the owner of half of the company shares but now I am having 25 percent of the shares", his father told him.

"Dad, I am grown up now. I am here to help you out. You don't need to worry", he said

His dad smiled with pride.

"The next week I am going to Bangalore for the interview", he told his dad

"Wish you all the best for the new opportunity son", he replied.

(They enjoyed the coffee and talked a little bit more)

Late at night, Akash reached home after work.

"Huff... what a hectic day!", He said to himself.

"Hello baby boy", his mother said.

"Hey, Mom" he replied.

"How are you, my son?" She asked.

" I am completely fine. What about you my beautiful mom? He asked.

"I am good. By the way, we are going to dinner. Do you want to join us?" She asked.

"Mom I am very much tired today. Is that okay if I go to my room to rest? He asked.

She shrugged. "Yeah, sure", she said.

He kissed his mother's hand and went to his room. He slept for a while. He had to recheck his presentation once again that's why he got up. Suddenly, he saw that a car had parked outside the house. It was Rahul. He was coming to see Akash's mother. Akash went downstairs to welcome him

"Where is my other mom? ", Rahul asked Akash's mother while greeting him.

"She went outside for dinner with Dad", Akash told him

"Ooo... Love doesn't die", he mocked

Akash punched him in his ribs to warn him.

Rahul replies, "Easy peasy bro, I was kidding".

"By the way, is she okay?", He asked

"Yeah, she is good but there are some family problems as well. Dad lost half of his shares of the company", he told him

"Really? How?", He asked with astonishment.

Akash then told him about the whole tragedy that happened with his dad. Rahul gave him more power by saying, "Their son has quite enough bank balance" he further said, "They don't need to worry about it".

"Yeah", I told Dad the same thing.

"I just remembered, when will you go to Bangalore?" Rahul asked with excitement.

"The day after tomorrow", he replied.

"I want to go with you there as well", Rahul told him about his plan.

"It would be great", he replied.

"Yes, we'll explore the city and celebrate your new journey of life", he told Akash about his long-term planning.

"Let me pass out the interview first. Don't make castles in the air", Akash advised.

(They both laughed)

"What about Shree?", Akash asked. "Her number is not available", he continued.

"I don't know Akash. I went to her home but I wasn't able to contact anyone from her family. I am worried for her", he said

The next day, they went shopping. They spent a whole day together because they were preparing to go to Bangalore. That night, Rahul got a call from his father. Rahul's father informed him that his cousin had died and they had to go to New York tomorrow on an early morning flight. Due to this reason, Rahul had to call off his plan with Akash.

He wished him good luck with his interview and left.

He knows that Akash will understand his situation.

The next day, Akash came downstairs, and his parents wished him good luck and took him to the airport. He was going to Bangalore by air. At the time of departure, they told him goodbye and went home.

Akash went to Bangalore.

All the arrangements were sponsored by the company. Akash had already qualified for the job with the top position so, the interview was just a formality. With all the protocols, Akash went to the company occupied by two buildings and had 25 floors in each. His interview went great as usual. But the moment of pride was the one when he got the joining letter.

"Mr. Akash welcome to our company", the CEO said.

"It's my pleasure to work here", Akash was thankful.

At that moment, he was so excited and a bit emotional too. He called his parents and told them that he got the job. For him, it was his dream to work in that company. His transition from an average working person to a hard-working professional helped him so much to get this job. He was thankful to God.

He was about to call Rahul but then he remembered that Rahul told him about his cousin's death. So, he didn't call him and sent the text. He was so happy that he updated the status on his Facebook profile. In the night, he had to go back to Delhi.

After taking some rest, he went to the airport. And within a few hours, he reached there. He stepped on the land with pride since he fulfilled his dream. It was no less than plucking the stars from the sky. As he reached his home, his parents decorated the house to give him a warm welcome back.

They wanted him to feel special that's why they arranged a small but beautiful welcome home party. They felt proud of their son.

They all enjoyed the dinner and had fun.

Akash went to his room and took a deep breath. He lay down on the bed to check his phone.

It has a lot of notifications. He read them all and felt proud.

He was so satisfied at the moment that he fell asleep within minutes. He had so many new things to face in his life. He was determined he would not miss the opportunity to fulfill his goals.

He usually had a habit of appreciating himself before going to sleep. That night he did the same thing and tried to keep himself motivated.

"There are so many things to come. Good luck Akash"

That day, Akash did the same thing, before going to sleep he told himself,

"Lack of direction, not lack of time, is the problem. We all have twenty-four hours in a day."

'A LEAP OF FAITH'

Staring into the void as the clouds rushed by, Akash was looking forward to working at his new workplace, thinking about his new beginning and his dream job. He remembered how he used to dream about this job and finally, his hard work and struggle had paid off.

As the plane began to slow down, Akash could feel butterflies in his stomach. "You have arrived at your destination" announced the flight attendant.

Akash all excited got up and picked up his luggage, ready to leave the airport. "This is it", he whispered to himself. As he left the airport, he was welcomed by a man in a suit holding a sign with his name written on it, who later drove him to his hotel.

Akash had arrived in Bangalore a few days in advance of his first day at work to familiarize himself with the new place and find an apartment. When he got to his room, he unpacked his stuff, took a shower, and laid down for the night.

It had been a long day for Akash but it was just the beginning. The next morning, he had a couple of days planned for apartment hunting. He had short-listed some of the places that he found most suitable. He spent his next few days looking for the perfect apartment, analyzing every single detail and scenario closely.

4 days later, he had finalized his decision and was all ready to move into his new place. He hired a moving company and shifted over to his new apartment.

This was a new beginning for Akash, which he had dreamt of for a long time. He stood in the middle of the room with his stuff scattered around, packed in moving boxes. Very excited and motivated, Akash started to unpack his belongings and set up his new apartment. He arranged his furniture and sorted his wardrobe.

After a while, Akash was all done.

"Now this feels more like home, but there is one thing missing", he thought to himself, he reached into his bag and pulled out a poster that had a motivational quote written across it that stated

"The harder I practice the luckier I get. ~ Gary Player" and hung it next to his mirror.

"Now it is complete", he said.

With his apartment all setup, Akash had a few days till his first day at the job. He decided to use those days to explore the city and visit its main attractions. He visited the Lalbagh Botanical Garden, the ISKCON Temple, and Tipu Sultan's Summer Palace.

These visits helped Akash relax and enjoy the city which he needed since he was tired from all the apartment hunting and setup. A day before his first day at his new job, he decided to prepare himself for his first day. Akash picked out his clothes for the next day and ironed them, all ready to wear. He then went over a few things that he thought would help him on his first day.

As the day passed by Akash became more and more nervous. Finally, it was nighttime, Akash went to bed early so that he was fresh in the morning. He took a shower, brushed his teeth, slid into his sleeping suit, and went to bed. Laying there on the bed filled with nervousness, Akash kept staring at the ceiling, imagining his first day. He just imagined how he would work and never lose sight of his focus on his goals until he came out at the top. Despite his best efforts, he could not get himself to sleep, he got up and drank a glass of warm milk to help him fall asleep.

The next morning, his alarm beeps as the sun's rays shine through the window. Akash jumped out of bed all excited and got ready for his first day. He took a shower, groomed himself, and dressed up for his first day.

After his breakfast, he leaves for the office. As his cab stops outside his new office, he tips the driver and gets out.

Akash just stood there staring at the building, he whispered to himself "Finally, what I wanted" and stepped inside.

He went to the counter desk and presented his ID. The clerk accompanied him to the waiting room. A few minutes later, a middle-aged guy in a suit walked him, Akas stood up and introduced himself while shaking his hand.

The person in the suit replied, "Hi, I am Roy. I will be your supervisor. It is nice to meet you. We have heard a lot of good things about you from your previous employers".

"It's a pleasure, I am looking forward to working with you," said Akash.

Roy then gave Akash, a tour of the office and showed him his office. Akash was feeling very accomplished as he stepped into the career journey of his dreams.

As he set up his desk he glanced outside his door and saw the office of the CEO. It had a big wall of windows and a great view of the city skyline. At that moment Akash started fantasizing about his future at this company as a CEO. He imagined what it would be like to have the respect of all his employees and how he would lead the company to new heights.

With this idea to help keep him motivated, Akash started his first day at his new workplace. Later that night Akash was feeling very satisfied with his new work environment and felt accomplished. He was excited to be living in a new city while working at his dream job, he shared his feelings of excitement for living in Bangalore on his social media and got a positive response from his friends and family. Many people suggested various things to try out which Bangalore was known for.

A couple of weeks after his first day, Akash was making great progress at his new workplace, fully committed to his work, working hard day and night with passion. He had built up great relations and a reputation at his company.

One afternoon Akash was getting ready for lunch, he was about to leave and his phone rang, it was Suhani. It had been a few months since they had talked.

They talked for a while and caught up on each other's lives. Suhani told him that she saw his post on social media about living in Bangalore and told him that she was living there as well for a while.

She suggested they meet up for lunch or dinner to catch up with each other properly. Akash agreed and they both decided to meet up for lunch the next day.

After a day, Akash went to the meetup point a bit early and was waiting for Suhani. After a while Suhani entered through the door wearing a black dress, as she approached Akash, he just stared at her for a few seconds stunned by her beauty. He suddenly shook his head slightly and stood up to greet Suhani. He pulled out a chair for Suhani to sit being a gentleman.

Once they were both seated, Suhani asked "So what brings you to Bangalore". Akash told her that he had just moved there about a month ago.

"I got an amazing opportunity; an opportunity of a lifetime and I knew I had to make it count," said Akash, told Suhani about how he got this job.

"This a job I have dreamt about for a long time and I never stopped working for it," he said.

Suhani replies, "You are one of those people who don't stop working until they have achieved their goal, I have always admired that about you".

Akash then asked Suhani about what she ended up in Bangalore, Suhani said "I was looking for a better job opportunity and applied in multiple companies, I got accepted in a few, one of which was Oracle and without any doubt, I accepted their job offer. I start this Monday. I will be working in the Human Resources department".

"Oracle!" Akash replied looking surprised, "That's where I work as well."

I just started around a month ago".

"That's amazing, finally a familiar face" replied Suhani gladly and with some relief.

"I was so nervous about starting over again at this new company, now it would be so much easier with you around". Akash smiled a nodded, "Yeah, it's a pleasant coincidence".

As they were sharing stories and thoughts a waiter came in and handed them the menu.

"I'm worked up and appetite, I need something to help me power through the day, I will have a Mexican chicken steak," said Akash.

Suhani continued "Just a plate of salad for me". They sat there exchanging old memories and catching up with each other.

Suhani told Akash "I was so nervous about moving here that I couldn't even finalize an apartment to live in, I still have to stay at a hotel".

In reply, Akash offered his help as a polite gesture. "That would be of great help. Thank you so much," said Suhani thanking Akash.

At that moment they both were glad to see a familiar person in this new city.

The next Monday, Akash was working at his office and the door knocked, he looked up and it was Suhani holding a desk plant. "This is for you," said Suhani.

"It's my first day and I thought to drop by and have a look at your office".

"Oh! That's right, you were supposed to start this Monday, I have been so busy that I almost forgot.

Please come in, have a seat" replied Akash.

"So how is your first day going?" asked Akash.

Suhani replies, "So far it is really good, I was nervous at first but everyone here is so nice and polite, I believe I enjoy working here".

"That is amazing," said Akash.

They sat there chatting for a few minutes.

"Well, I should get back to my office," said Suhani and left. Akash could feel attracted towards Suhani, by the way, she dressed and always kept herself upright but always suppressed his feelings.

He never allowed himself to be distracted by these feelings ever since his last breakup, he used to distract himself by staying focused on his career.

Later that day as Akash was leaving for home, it was Suhani standing outside and waiting for a cab. He offered to drop her. As she approached his car, Akash went ahead and opened the car door for her. They both got in the car and were on their way back home.

"Would you like some music?" asked Akash, "Sure" replied Suhani.

Akash put up some Indian songs for Suhani. He remembered that she likes Indian songs from a few years back at Rahul's party when Suhani asked him to play some desi songs instead of Western music.

"Oh! I love this song" said Suhani "I am surprised you remembered what I liked".

Akash smirked and nodded slightly. Suhani was impressed by the politeness and the gentle nature of Akash.

She felt drawn towards him. Since Suhani and Akash were old friends, they used to hang out all the time and started to enjoy each other's company a lot.

They used to meet randomly for lunch, dinners, and even movies.

After a couple of months, Suhani started to fall for Akash. She used to tell her friends about Akash and told them that she was attracted to him. The thought of telling Akash about her feelings had crossed her mind multiple times but she never found the right moment.

After a while, she planned that she would invite Akash to a movie and tell him everything. She picked up the phone and called Akash.

"Hi, Suhani, what's up?" Akash answered.

"There a new Tom Hardy movie coming out, you want to watch it?" asked Suhani, she knew that Tom was one of his favorite celebrities.

"Of course! I like his movies," said Akash.

"Okay great! I'll book two tickets for this Friday" Suhani said full of excitement.

She went and booked two tickets for the new Tom Hardy movie. Later that day she talked to her friend, Sara, about her decision to tell Akash everything during the movies. Sara knew that Akash was a person who was always focused on his career and would not be interested in Suhani which would break her heart.

She tried to talk Suhani out of her plan, "Have you thought this through?" asked Sara "Are you sure you want to tell him about everything?".

Suhani replies, "We have been friends for years and he has always been so polite to me and I mean extra polite. I cannot help but think that he likes me too but would not tell me about it.".

Sara was afraid that her decision would break her heart and continued to convince her not to move forward with her plan.

"Suhani looks, Akash is a person whose career means everything to him. He works day and night motivated to achieve only one goal" she explained,

"What if he doesn't feel the same way about you? This could ruin your friendship. You guys have been friends for so long and he is the only old friend you have in this city, are you willing to risk it all." Sara continued to convince her.

She made some excellent points that caused Suhani to have a major dilemma. After some more convincing, Sara was able to talk Suhani out of telling Akash about her feelings.

Finally, it was Friday. Suhani and Akash met outside the cinema. "Excited for this movie," said Akash while Suhani stood there trying her best to hold herself back from telling Akash about everything.

As she was rethinking her decision over and over again, Akash said "It is about to start, 'let's go."

At that moment Suhani snapped herself out of her thoughts and decided to just watch the movie for the night. After the movie, Akash was in a good mood.

He suggested, "I'm starving, let's get something to eat, and then we'll head home.".

Suhani smiled and nodded wishing she could tell Akash what she felt. They went to the nearest restaurant and ordered some food.

"You have been quiet, is everything all right?" asked Akash.

Suhani in her heart wished "Oh you have no idea. I wish I could tell you", she thought to herself.

"It is nothing, just work, I don't think I am well suited for this job and I don't know if I can keep up with it."

This had Akash concerned, he wanted Suhani to keep working there, and he loved her company.

"Oh! Why is that?" asked Akash, "Nothing, I just feel a bit overwhelmed by everything".

Akash tried to comfort and encourage and motivate her to work harder for it, "You are a very talented person, Suhani, I believe you are the right person for this job" he said, "There are ups and downs in every aspect of life, but that doesn't mean that you cannot overcome those challenges and face your problems, you just have to work a bit harder, you will come out even stronger and more motivated than before."

Akash continued to comfort her. At this moment Akash could not let Suhani go, he felt so comfortable around her but still had kept his friendship to a limit.

After his last breakup, he never let anyone get close to him, but maybe this was time, and maybe it was a chance to move on and take a leap of faith in others once more. He gathered courage and shared his personal family experiences with Suhani.

"I learned a lot of things from my father, one of those things is to never stop fighting no matter how bad the odds seem," said Akash, "My father suffered a great loss in his career, but he never stopped working, he never gave up. Whenever I feel overwhelmed, I just think of my father and try to imagine what he would do."

This was the first time Akash had ever shared his personal family story with anyone. Although it was not much, Akash felt a wave of relief after opening up about his matters.

"That felt good, baby steps," Akash thought to himself.

Suhani smiled; she was glad that they were at a point in their friendship where Akash felt so comfortable with her that he shared something so personal with her. At that moment she had finalized her decision of not talking about her feelings with Akash.

She doesn't want to jeopardize the friendship they had.

She realized that she was the only one, Akash had in Bangalore with whom he could talk and share his troubles. She knew she could count on him.

She tried her best to stop her heart, leaning towards Akash. But it wasn't ready for that. She decided to impress Akash so that he could find her as a perfect match for him.

She was now determined to become more closer to him.

The next day, Suhani decides to make something for Akash to impress him. She knew that she wasn't a perfect cook, not even close to it so she decided to make something light and healthy. So, she went to the market. Suhani bought some vegetables from the market and prepared a Salad for him.

She thought that it would help her get some idea about his taste in food.

That day during lunchtime, she went to Akash's office.

"Knock, knock", she knocked at the door

"Come in", Akash said in a loud voice.

"Oh, Suhani. Please come", he said

"Hello", she replied.

"Is everything okay? You didn't inform me before coming here", he asked.

"Oh, I am sorry. I wanted to give you a surprise", she said

"I am not surprised", he said.

"Anyways, I made something for you," she said

"Something for me? What is it?" He asked.

"Vegetable salad, light and healthy, perfect for lunch. Here it is", she said

He laughed

"What?", Suhani asked.

"At least you should've asked me before going to make this", he said.

"Don't you like it?", She said

" I don't like Vegetables Suhani", he told her

"Oh, I didn't know it", she said in a low voice

"That's why I am saying that you should've asked me first" he justified.

"Now?", She said.

"Now, go and make something non-veg for me", he said.

Now Suhani has an idea about his taste in food.

"Did you have your lunch?", She asked.

"Not yet", he replied

"Do you want to accompany me at lunch?", She asked.

"Am... Not today, Suhani. I am really busy. I have a lot of work to do. We will plan something for the weekend", he said while working on his laptop.

"But you should also care about your diet", she advised.

"I'll manage it. But for now, please let me work", he replied in a hurry.

"Okay, see you soon", she replied.

In the evening, she went outside the office. She thought that Akash would be there. She was sure that Akash would drop her home but Akash was in a rush and left the office without considering that Suhani was waiting for him. She was hurt but couldn't do anything. She took a cab then and went to her place.

Now she was realizing why Sara stopped her from leaning towards Akash. "Huff... That man is a workaholic", she said to herself.

She thought that someday she would change Akash but she had to do so much struggle for that change. She was determined to work on it but she needed patience as well.

Suhani was very sensitive. And gradually she was also becoming sensitive to Akash. She didn't like other girls to get frank with Akash. Although, she had nothing to do with that still she got hurt whenever Akash talked to other girls in a friendly manner or went with them outside the office for lunch and hangouts.

Somehow, she waited for the whole week. She wants to plan a movie night with him.

She reminded Akash that they have a weekend plan. On Friday, she called Akash and asked him about the meet-up.

"Movie? This weekend?", She asked

"Yeah, sure", he replied.

Saturday night was decided for the movie.

Suhani invites Akash to her apartment for the movie. Akash went to her place, and they watched the movie.

"Did you enjoy it?" Suhani asked.

"Of course... I enjoyed" Akash replies.

Akash didn't notice that much but Suhani looked confused.

After the movie, they talked about some random stuff from their daily routine. Suhani was happy that she had Akash in her life.

Now, she has to plan her next move.

CHAPTER NINE

'AFFAIR OF THE HEART: ANOTHER VALENTINE'

"And this is how my dad lost some of his business shares", Akash told the recent family trauma to Suhani.

"What is he doing now?" She asked him.

"He has some shares left in the business. He is trying to get back his position", he told her.

"Don't worry, everything will be okay", she once again comforted Akash.

(Akash shrugged)

Suhani was so attracted to Akash. Despite his average looks, he had a charming personality which drew Suhani towards him. Akash was a career-focused person but, he also felt attracted to Suhani. He was still ambiguous about his feelings for Suhani but he was good at distracting himself towards his career too.

"Oh, it is so much cold here", Suhani said.

She had forgotten her jacket at the apartment, and now she was shivering from the cold. Akash was feeling a bit selfish so he gave his jacket to Suhani to put on.

"That's sweet" " she said and smiled.

"Take it and for the next time, don't forget your jacket or sweater at least", he advised.

They both went outside the coffee shop and walked towards the apartments. They had so many shops right near to their office and apartment, so they usually visited there by walking.

"Thank you for the jacket", Suhani said.

"My pleasure", Akash replies.

Akash moved towards the male block of the building, and Suhani went to her side. While she still had Akash's jacket over her shoulder.

"Ah! What an amazing scent", she complimented Akash on his choice of fragrance.

She once again fell in love with him. She texted him,

"I like the fragrance by the way". (Along with some heart emoji)

Akash didn't reply to her because he didn't want to give her any hint about his feelings for her. He just wanted to hide them from her because he wasn't ready for new trauma.

She waited for his reply, but she didn't get the answer. At last, she sent him a good night text and went to sleep.

The next day, Akash replied to her.

"Sorry, I didn't see your messages. I fell asleep".

Suhani replied to him, "Good Morning".

Akash thought that now it would be rude to ignore her morning wishes so he decided to text her back.

"Good morning my friend".

"Hmm... friend", she replied.

Akash ignored her message now. He didn't want to distract himself because he knew how much he struggled to bring him into this new lifestyle.

"Beep", his phone vibrated again.

Suhani again texted him, "See you soon".

Akash was waiting for his Boss as he had to give a presentation on a very new project. He was working keenly on that project for the last two weeks and finally, he was about to present the whole project in front of the project holders.

Suhani was waiting outside for Akash.

"Where are you?", she texted him.

He was working on the project with alacrity. He was not ready to miss the bulletin making his position more lucrative in the office. He also knew that he was the major breadwinner of the family. He was not dependent on his father's earnings after high school.

Suhani waited for him but he was very busy working. She was about to knock on the door but Akash's workmate told her that he doesn't like anyone to disturb him. She stopped herself and didn't knock on the door.

"Suhani, are you coming with me?" her friend asked her to accompany her during lunch.

"Yeah, sure", she replied.

(Suhani put the jacket of Akash in the cabinet)

They both went to the office café for lunch.

She was a friend of Suhani. They used to talk and share stuff.

"Are you okay?", she asked Suhani.

"Yeah, I'm good", she replied.

(She was eating rice with daal but his focus was Akash only. She was thinking about his behavior as it was no more ambivalent to her that Akash was ignoring her)

"Suhani?", she poked Suhani.

"Hah", Suhani replied unconsciously.

"What are you thinking about? What is bothering you?", she asked again

"Nothing" (with a pause), nothing at all", she answered.

"Are you thinking about Akash?", her friend asked her.

"Yeah, he is ignoring me I guess", she complained.

"Suhani, I warned you already. He is a career-focused man. He got a promotion within six months. Can you imagine that?", she told her.

"It is useless to run after him", She advised her.

(They finished their food. Suhani was still in the deep thoughts)

Suhani was using her phone when she collided with Akash. He had a coffee in his hand that toppled down on Akash's hand.

"WHAT THE HELL", Akash didn't see that it was Suhani and yelled.

"Excuse ...", Suhani was about to retaliate but she stopped herself when she saw Akash.

"I am sorry", She apologized

"What's wrong with you lady?", Akash asked

"I didn't see you. I was looking at my phone", she replied.

"Ugh...", Akash complained and went to the parking.

Suhani was looking at him. She frowned. She went straight to her room and started crying.

She decides to never text him again, but she is so helpless due to her feelings for him.

Akash, on the other, didn't want to associate himself once again with someone. He was in Bangalore to work for his ambitions of life but it was hard for him because deep down in his heart, he was also attracted towards Suhani.

That day, Suhani didn't text him at all. She didn't even come for the coffee as well. Staring at the walls, she was thinking about Akash.

"From the day, he opened the door of the car for her until today, I always had him in my mind", she told herself. She grabbed her phone and stared at the pictures of Akash. She wanted to tell him about her feelings for him but she was scared of losing a friend as well.

"Suhani?", her roommate was knocking at the door.

(She fell asleep while looking at the pictures of Akash)

Her roommate called Akash and told him that Suhani had locked herself in the room. Akash came to the building and they tried to open her room. Luckily, an extra key was available and they were able to enter the room.

She was sleeping on the carpet right next to her bed. Her phone was lying aside. Akash went forward to poke her; he saw his pictures on her phone. That moment melted Akash's heart.

He then realized how much serious she was for her. Akash left her room to control himself.

"Suhani?", her friends poked her

She got up and replied, "What's wrong?"

"Why did you lock the door? We were so upset Suhani", she said.

"We?", she asked with confusion.

"Yes, Akash was there. I called him because you weren't unlocking the door. I got scared about you that's why I called him", she told her.

Suhani's heart missed a beat, "Was he worried for me?", She asked.

"Worried? He was very worried for you Suhani", her friend told her.

"But you did a great stupidity", Suhani said to her roommate.

"I was scared", She replied

Suhani thought that her friend bothered Akash for no reason, so she decided to apologize to him.

"Are you free tonight?", She texted Akash.

Sitting in the park, listening to the songs, he lost himself in deep thoughts. The Park was full of people, he was staring at the tree in front of him. While staring at the tree, he got Suhani's call. He brought his mobile out of his pocket and checked his phone.

"Suhani's call", he asked himself.

He was unable to make up his mind. He was as clear as mud. He once again tried to ignore her.

"Why are you throwing me off Suhani?", he said to himself.

Akash started liking her but he had so many more things to do as well.

He can't afford to be distracted again. It took him a long time to gather himself after his breakup with Anshu.

That's why he was very scared.

Suhani texted him, "Please pick up the call".

This unexpected behavior of Akash was throwing her off balance. She called him again.

"Yes, Suhani?", he picked up the call.

"Where were you? I was calling you", she replied.

"I am busy right now. I'll let you know when I'll get free", he was trying to get rid of the situation.

"I am waiting for your call", she said and disconnected the call.

She spent the whole day in her room, waiting for Akash's call. She was thrown for the loop when he saw Akash's new updated status on WhatsApp. She was broken into pieces when she realized that Akash was lying to her. She understood that Akash wanted to get rid of her. She had become a clingy girl because she wanted to be a part of

Akash's life. But Akash's ignorance which was accidentally on purpose was now adding fuel to the flames.

Laying on the bed, spreading out her hair, she was staring at the ceiling of her room. She closed her eyes and started thinking about Akash.

"I wish I could tell you my feelings for you", she thought to herself and tears were all in her eyes.

Meanwhile, her phone rang and she opened her eyes in a jiffy. She thought that it must be Akash and yes it was Akash.

"Hello, Yes Suhani, I just got free", He said

(His voice was so exotic that it always melted Suhani's heart)

She was angry with him but she responded to him with her normal behavior.

"Oh, okay", she replied.

"Do you want to have a meet-up tonight?", he asked

"Yeah! Sure", she replied

"So, dinner?", he asked

She blushed and said, "Yes".

They both then disconnected the call. Suhani was so excited, that she thought that she would tell Akash about her feelings today.

She opened up her wardrobe and tried to find the perfect dress for tonight's dinner. She wanted to look perfect tonight. She didn't find a good dress to impress him so she went out shopping. She got a beautiful black dress from the market. She wanted to cut the dash at today's dinner.

Akash was not concerned about tonight's dinner. He was just meeting her because she wanted to talk to him.

"It's 8 O'clock. Let's go for dinner now", he said himself

"Are you coming?", he texted her

"Of course! I am even about to reach the venue", she replied within a minute.

When Akash went to the venue, he saw Suhani, striking with her beauty. She was looking perfectly a hair out of place. Akash went outside his car and approached her

"Hello lady", he said

"Hi, you are still late as always", she replied.

"And you looked like a dollar just like always", He complimented.

(She blushed and shrugged)

They both went to the rooftop.

"It's a pleasure to have you, Sir Akash. What can I help you with? What would you like to order today?" The waiter came to them to take their order.

"I'll go with salad", she ordered.

"Salad?", Akash mocked.

"Yeah, I am a vegetarian", She told Akash.

"I'll go with the Chicken Malai Boti with lemonade" he ordered.

"Okay, thank you for joining us once again sir, your food will be served within 20 minutes", the waiter replied to them.

Suhani was about to ask something when the waiter interrupted them again

"Sorry to interrupt you ma'am, but would you like me to serve you Salad with Mr. Akash's food, or do you want it before that", the waiter asked.

Suhani looked at Akash and said,

"Serve the salad with food".

The waiter said, "Okay ma'am" and went to the kitchen.

"Why vegetables only?", Akash asked

"Because I love to eat them more than other food items", she replied.

"Okay, Cool", he replied.

"The waiter knows you very well, I think you often come here", she asked.

"Yes, I have many memories here", he replied.

He was looking at Suhani because her beauty was affecting Akash's mood.

'Black color suits you a lot. You know that right", he said.

"Thank you", she said and smiled.

"I still remember the day when I picked you up for Rahul's birthday party. On that day, you were dressed to the nine", he said

"Oh really, I thought you didn't notice", she said

"What's the date today?", He asked

"Umm... It is 10th of February", she said

"I gave you a compliment on your beauty back than one year and three months ago", Aakash reminded her.

"Hahaha... impressive, you are pretty good in mathematics", she smiled and mocked.

"Yes, I am good at mathematics", he said.

She thought that it would be Valentine's Day right ahead after 4 days. She thought that she shouldn't tell him about her feelings today.

She can propose to him on Valentine's Day. So, she made up her mind and tried not to remind Akash why are they meeting at the moment.

"By the way, you wanted to talk to me about something?", Akash asked.

"I am... For nothing", she replied.

Akash was looking at his phone. He thought that Suhani didn't listen to him because he was looking at his phone.

He insisted, "Tell me, I am listening".

She decides to confuse him. She wants to know his reaction if she will tell him that she is in love with someone.

"I am here to tell you something", she said

"Okay", Akash said

"I wanted you to give me your best opinion", she said.

"All right, what is it?", he said.

She was about to say but the waiter came with the food.

"Hmmm... what an amazing smell, Bon appetite", he said.

"Here is your food sir", the waiter served the Malai Boti to Akash.

"And here is your Salad Ma'am", the waiter served the salad to Suhani

He served the food and said,

"Enjoy your meal".

"Malai Boti always makes me mouthful", Akash said.

"Looks like you are in love with chicken", she said

"Correct", he replied

He started eating his food as he was hungry.

Suhani was also having her salad.

"By the way, what were we talking about?", Akash asked

"I am in love with a person completely different from my personality", she told him.

He stopped eating and looked at her face.

"You are what?", he said.

"Really?", Suhani said.

"Didn't hear you? You are in love?", he said.

"Well, good for you", he also complimented right after that.

(She shrugged)

"Now as a friend, what would you suggest?", she asked

"I don't know. It's completely up to you", he said

A silence took place during the dinner. Akash's mood was almost spoiled when Suhani told him about her situation.

"You're a good catch, Suhani, ask yourself first while taking any decision", he mitigated the silence.

"Hmm... so are you", she said unconsciously.

Akash laughed

They both finished their food and Suhani told Akash that she was getting late. She wanted to go home

"Okay, I can drop you home if you want", Akash said

"No, it's okay. I am a pretty independent woman. I'll manage it on my own", she replied

Akash raised his eyebrows and said,

"Okay... ".

(Suhani took the cab and left the restaurant)

Akash also went to the parking to get his car and left the restaurant.

On the way home, he was just thinking about Suhani. It was the first time in his life after his breakup that he thought about a girl in that serious way.

(He sighed)

In the middle of the way towards his home, Akash stopped the car in front of the mall. He has to buy some groceries for the coming week. The mall was a complete departmental store. He was passing by the one corner of the store specified for books and stationery. He randomly saw the tag "Latest Books". He went to that area and started looking at the books.

"Damn... It's an ocean of knowledge", he said.

He was looking for some productive books. But then he was suggested by the shopkeeper that he should read Forty Rules of Love by Elif Shafak. It was the first time when someone suggested something to read. He was not sure whether he had properly read it before or not. It was his first favorite book he read in Delhi so, he decided to read it again in Bangalore.

"Where is Forty Rule...", he asked the shopkeeper.

"Yeah, right there", he was searching the book.

He bought that book and was excited to read it again. Other than that, he bought some of the groceries which reminded him of Shree.

"Ah, it's been so long. I didn't even see her", he said himself.

He missed her sister many times but due to his workload, he didn't get time to call her or visit her. She also didn't contact him and went missing.

He did some grocery and went back to the apartment.

He was about to sleep when he checked his phone.

"Thank you for the dinner", Suhani texted him.

He ignored her message and checked the other message. He had been in search of a house in Bangalore for the past few days. So, he got a message from a property dealer that he got a reasonable house for him.

"Tomorrow, get some time and visit the house", the property dealer texted him

He was excited for the next day because he wanted to have his property in Bangalore.

He looked at Suhani's message again. He replied to her back with a smile emoji.

The next day, Suhani went to the office. She visited Akash's office but he wasn't there. She came to know that Akash was on leave today. She got worried and was about to text him but she stopped herself. And went to her floor.

"Is he okay?", She asked herself.

"He never missed his office. Work is everything for him", she again thought.

On the other hand, Akash visited the house. It was a perfect house for him. He was so happy to get something that was perfect for him. Every corner of the house was complete according to his taste.

"It's a done deal", he said to the dealer.

He was feeling so happy and proud of himself at that moment.

"Hey, Rahul guess what?", He called Rahul to give him this news.

"Did Suhani propose you?", he said and laughed loudly

"Oh, shut up, Rahul", he groaned

He then told him about his property, the house of his dream in Bangalore. Rahul was happy for him

After three days, Akash got a message from Suhani.

"Today's dinner from my side", Akash read her message and replied, "Okay!"

It was Valentine's Day, and Suhani wanted to propose to Akash on that day. Akash was usually dressed up to the nines. He went to the given venue. He completely forgot that it was Valentine's Day because he had been working on his project's presentation with alacrity for the past few days.

He saw the Red Balloons all over the restaurant and he remembered that it was Valentine's Day. He was feeling so uncomfortable but then Suhani appeared in front of him.

She was once again struck with her beauty

"Here you are", he said Suhani

"Yes, here I am", she replied.

She was in a happy mood, but she was feeling butterflies in her stomach. After all, she was about to propose to Akash. He wanted to share her feelings with him.

"Come with me", she said.

They both went to the rooftop.

It was decorated beautifully with Red and White Balloons. He saw the big heart-shaped board with I LOVE YOU AKASH.

Akash looked around himself and tried to get the point. "What is it?", he asked.

Suhani bent her knees down and proposed to Akash.

"Will you, be my valentine?", she said full of nervousness but she was determined too.

"What are you doing Suhani?", he was feeling embarrassed in front of everyone.

"Please get up, stop doing this. I am feeling so bad", he admonished.

People around them were clapping and hooting. They were encouraging the love birds to express their love.

"Say yes, say yes, say yes", all of the other people including the staff encouraged Akash to say yes.

Akash was at sixes and seven in the restaurant.

"Please, answer me Akash", she requested.

Akash didn't say anything. He put his hand on her shoulders and helped her to stand up on her legs.

Suhani was asking for the answer. Akash made her comfortable and gave her a glass of water.

The area was now a bit clear, and they were almost alone on the rooftop.

"Suhani, I didn't think like that about us", he said

"But I love you so much Akash", she said

Akash wanted to get rid of the situation. Suhani was crying, and Akash didn't want to leave her like this. He said,

"All right, at least give me some time to think about it."

CHAPTER TEN

'THE NEW OUTSET'

"Every true love and friendship is a story of unexpected transformation. If we are the same person before and after we love, that means we haven't loved enough", he read this line while reading a renounced book named FORTY RULES OF LOVE.

After his first breakup, Akash used to spend some time reading books. Luckily, he got the answers to all the questions circulating in his mind. He decided to put himself first and start a new beginning in life.

"What if I found Suhani more compatible than Anshu in this new journey", he asked himself.

Not only this, he had already discussed Suhani's proposal with Shree and Rahul. Being his honest buddies, they gave him a very positive response about the new proposal and motivated him to go for it. Yet he didn't make up his mind. He took a deep breath and asked himself to make a good judgment about the proposal. But his mind was completely crowded with the memory, the memories he had with Anshu when they were in a relationship.

He thought a lot about the proposal of Suhani and decided to tell her about his past first. He wanted to start everything in a pure manner.

He doesn't want any ambiguity at the outset of life, and that's why he decided to put himself to tell Suhani about his past and his relationship.

But also, he was worried about the response from Suhani after telling her the truth.

The next day, he went to the office and tried to keep himself at work but he wasn't able to distract himself from Suhani's cabin since her cabin was right in front of his cabin.

While staring at her cabin, Suhani appeared in front of him and said,

"Hello!".

"Akash?", she asked him again.

He was looking in deep thought while staring at Suhani's cabin. Suhani poked him once again.

"Ah, yes?" he replied unconsciously.

"What happened Akash? Are you okay? You don't seem good. Is everything all right?" she inquired him in a worry.

"Yes, I am good Suhani. How are you?" he simply answered and said that he was a bit busy right now and couldn't talk to her.

Suhani got worried.

She thought that her proposal disturbed him. She went to her cabin. Not to mention, she was demotivating herself for proposing to his workmate.

On the other hand, Akash started his daily work but multiple thoughts were still disturbing him. He went to the café for a cup of tea and asked Suhani if she wanted to accompany him. They both went to the office café.

"I don't know how to explain my thoughts to you but I have so much to tell you", Akash said.

Suhani comforted him and said, "You can share with me anything, right!"

Akash told her about his past relationship with Anshu and he also added that he might not be able to give her all the happiness she deserves.

Suhani placed her hand on his hand and comforted him that she had nothing to do with his past and ready to accept everything. Akash had already been impressed by Suhani's personality and now after hearing this, he was super comfortable.

Then they got back to work. They both looked a bit relaxed after having a small conversation in the cafe.

Akash decided to answer the proposal of Suhani at dinner. He wanted to make it a surprise. That's why before leaving the office, he asked Suhani to meet him at home for dinner. She was all ready to accept his invitation.

"I can't wait. I'll be there on time", she said and smiled.

"I'll wait for you then", Akash said and left the office.

Akash decided to arrange a beautiful dinner for her. He chose the poolside of her house for dinner and decorated the whole sight with beautiful red flowers and balloons.

He did so because people really celebrate their proposal this way and also, he wanted to give her a surprise. Not only this, but he also wanted to express his feelings in such a beautifully decorated romantic way. He was so excited because it would be a very new beginning for him.

Soon after completing the decoration and preparation of the dinner, he dressed nicely. He put some fragrance too and went downstairs to re-check everything. When he was coming downstairs, he heard the voice of a car's engine.

Suddenly, the bell rang. He looked at the time and asked himself in a hurry, "It must be Suhani"

He gave a last look at all the decorations and went to open the door. It was Suhani.

"Hi! You look good Akash" she said with excitement.

"Hello! And you're looking beautiful than ever" he nicely admired her.

He let her in and took her towards the pool sight where she was surprised after looking at the beautiful romantic decoration. She had tears in her eyes and then Akash said,

"I wanted to make you feel special Suhani," he said in a teary voice, "I want to tell you that I love you so much", he added.

Suhani hugged him and cried with happiness. Meanwhile, Akash made her feel comfortable. And he took her to the dining table and wiped her tears off. Suhani was delighted that Akash had accepted her proposal and he responded to me in such a beautiful way.

They had their dinner and talked a lot about their worthwhile moments. They planned new things and enjoyed the whole scenario. They both were so happy.

They expressed their love over and over and spent the whole night beautifully and they made a promise to each other not to leave. That's what people do during experiencing such moments.

And this is how Akash and Suhani were out setting the new journey of life after being accepted the reality of their past.

Of course, a new journey has new rules. There are always modern solutions to modern problems. So, by keeping all the things about the relationship in their minds, Akash and Suhani made some rules and regulations to make their relationship more everlasting and stronger. Akash needed to work on him more than Suhani since she was a calm and polite girl in nature.

Akash was still not able to have control over his temperament. They decided to go on their first date where they could enjoy and discuss all the things.

So, the next weekend, they went on their first date at The Leela Palace as it is the most renowned palace there. They spent a whole day and discussed their goals and achievements in life. Not only this, but they also shared detailed information about their families and other close friends.

"My parents are so supportive in all matters", Akash told her. "They never forced me about anything in my life until now, they've always supported me as they are very attached to me emotionally" he added.

Suhani was glad to hear that his parents were emotionally attached to him. She told him about her parents and became a bit upset.

"When I was at the age of 10, my parents got separated. And soon after they divorced each other", she said.

Akash seemed a bit sad for her but he then held her hand and made her ease her grief, he said, "It's life, my beautiful lady, you don't need to be sad about it. This is what god had decided for them" he hold her hand more tightly now. Suhani was so happy to have Akash as a life partner since he understood Suhani's position in the right manner. They both were now deeply attached. They decided to live together.

At first, they thought that they worked in the same place and now they are in a relationship so it would be appropriate to live together in the same house and same place. They both agreed on it since there was no family pressure on them at all.

Suhani was not as perfect as Akash considered her at first, as nobody is perfect in this world, she also has some flaws like she wasn't that good in-house holding stuff.

She didn't even cook anything in her life. Akash was expecting so many things but he compromised over a lot of things as well. But still how much compromises helped them in having an everlasting relationship.

Akash gave plenty of time to Suhani to make her realize that she should be responsible in the house holding stuff from now on. But since Suhani was a working woman, she didn't get his point and completely considered herself out of the house-holding responsibility.

"Have you seen my blue shirt?" Akash asked Suhani while digging all the stuff out of the cupboard.

"No, honey I don't even know that you have a blue shirt as well," she said carelessly.

"Really?" Akash asked surprisingly. "Can you help me find it out? I am getting late Suhani" he requested

"I am also getting late. I have a very important meeting today" she said in a hurry and left the room.

Akash controlled himself and didn't say anything. He simply put on another shirt and went downstairs.

Akash's friends advised that he has to be calm every time to make this relationship compatible, so he did the same. That's why he was compromising about all the things. When he came downstairs, he went to the kitchen to get something for breakfast but he was astonished to know that there was nothing for breakfast. The kitchen was messed up. He once again tried to cool himself down. And he went for the office in an irritable state of mind.

Then he came to the office and was about to start his work when he got a notification. It was Suhani's text.

"I'll be late at home today. Don't wait for me at dinner." The notification that appeared.

"Okay", Akash simply replies.

From entering the office to the moment he left the office, he was completely in distress. He wanted to get some relief. So, he called his friend Rahul and asked him to have a meet-up tonight.

"I am pretty disturbed; I need someone to talk to. Can we meet up?" he sent Rahul, a message.

Since Rahul was so close to him and also working in Bangalore. That's why he replied to Akash promptly and they decided to meet.

Akash directly went to Rahul's place. He was so completely in a state of distress that he hugged his friend and told him that he couldn't understand whether is it good for him or not.

"What are you talking about?" asked Rahul.

"I am talking about my relationship with Suhani", Akash said in a frustrated way.

"What's wrong Akash?" he inquired him in worry.

"I don't know why is it so hard for Suhani to understand her responsibilities," he told him.

"Look at me man, put yourself up. Why are you so worried about it now?" Rahul tried to comfort him.

Akash explained to him the whole problem he was facing being in a relationship with Suhani. He told Rahul that he did his best to calm himself. He was working so much on his temper but the Suhani wasn't able to get my point. He said that he loved Suhani so much he didn't want to lose her. He wanted to make this relationship everlasting but Suhani was not taking it seriously, she was being irresponsible in so many things.

Rahul said, "Did you talk to her?"

"No, I didn't," Akash said in a disappointed tone.

Rahul calmed him down and offered him something to drink.

"Let's have our dinner first, then we will talk about it," Rahul told Akash.

On the other, Suhani reached home. And when he didn't find Akash at home. She waited first and then texted him.

"Where are you?", she sent Akash, a message.

Akash read her message and simply ignored it because he didn't want to argue with her right now. He was enjoying his meal with his best friend Rahul.

Meanwhile, Suhani was waiting for Akash's reply but she didn't get any reply from him. She was worried about him and called him. Akash loved her so much and that's when he was about to pick up her call but unfortunately due to low battery, his mobile shut down. He then got busy talking to Rahul.

Suhani got more worried about Akash. She got angry as well since Akash didn't tell her about his plan.

"So, how was the food?", Rahul asked.

"It was great, my friend," Akash said with pleasure.

Rahul simply came closer to him and patted his shoulder and said, "Go and talk to her about your problems". Akash understood and he decided to shore up his relationship with Suhani by using all the ways.

When he was about to leave Rahul's place. He advised Akash,

"Relationships last not because they were destined to last. Relationships last long because two people choose to work for it."

"Hmm, thank you Rahul", Akash said in a way that he was so blessed to have such an amazing friend.

Suhani was worried for Akash because it was already midnight and he didn't even come home. She was so angry with him and waited for him anxiously. When Akash came back home, Suhani started screaming at him and doubtfully inquired him. She also complained to him about why he was not picking up her phone and not even texting her back. Not only this, she was so angry with him that he snatched him from his shirt's collar and inquired him where was he all night. This dissatisfied behavior made Akash so mad that he almost lost his temper and then started complaining about Suhani's irresponsibility. They both were arguing badly. It was their first fight after being in a relationship.

The whole fight made them disappointed and with the arguments made, Suhani started crying. When Akash realized that her eyes were full of tears, he stopped himself and hugged Suhani. He asked her not to cry like this because he couldn't see her cry just because of an argument.

"Okay, relax", Akash said. "Sit here and calm down please" he added.

She was sobbing so badly. Akash got some water for her to drink. He apologized for being so harsh during the argument. He sat down near Suhani and tried to talk to her calmly.

"Suhani, there are so many things I want to tell you. I wanted to get off my chest because I love you so much", Akash said politely. "I want you to understand these things, I don't want to lose you, please listen to me" he continued to explain.

Akash continued to explain everything about how he felt being in a relationship with her. He simply made her realize that they have to live together for the rest of their lives and they can't ignore their responsibilities. He told her that he wanted her to be responsible for doing household stuff. He also assured her that he wasn't burdening her by doing all the stuff alone. He cleared her that he wanted them to be responsible for making this house a more worthwhile living place for themselves.

"We need to fix our problem instead of ignoring each other", Akash said.

They both were in tears since they loved each other. That's why they gave some space to each other and took some time to make things good for themselves. It was a terrible night for both of them but it proved as a milestone for both of them.

"Oh, it's 10 O'clock" Akash got up and asked himself in a hurry.

He got ready for the office and came downstairs. He went to the kitchen and today he was astonished once again that the kitchen was nicely cleaned by someone, of course, who else could do this. (Except Suhani)

Not only this, he got a note on the front door of the refrigerator,

"I made your favorite sandwich for breakfast and placed it in the oven. Go and enjoy your breakfast"

It made Akash so happy that he almost forgot that he was getting late for the office and enjoyed his breakfast made by her beloved lady, Suhani. Although she wasn't an expert, she at least tried to cook something for his man. This all made him realize that he would now give more respect and love to her.

Then Akash decided not to go office on that day. He cleaned their room as well and made his promise true that he would be responsible too for making this house a worthy living place. After completing his home task, he called Suhani but she was busy and didn't find time to pick up the call. So left a text with a message,

"Thank you for such an amazing breakfast, it was so delicious to have such an amazing sandwich made by your honey." (Along with love emojis)

"There is a surprise for you as well", he texted this as well.

After an hour, when Suhani read Akash's messages, she simply replied with "Okay". But she was also suspicious about the surprise.

"Hmm...What it would be now?" she asked herself.

In the evening, when she got back home. She was expecting something like their proposal night from Akash but there was nothing special at all. The whole house was cleaned and everything was well settled. No doubt, that gave her an amazing vibe. Anyways she went upstairs. She was about to change her clothes when she saw an envelope on the side table. She took it and read her name on it.

"Dear Suhani! Please open" the pre-written message on the envelope. She opened the envelope and was astonished to see the tickets for a trip to Bali. She got a huge smile on her face and right after that Akash appeared and asked her about the surprise. She was so happy that she hugged him and said,

"You always made me surprised like this".

Akash laughed and said with love, "You deserve these surprises".

They both once again looked so happy and satisfied with each other. They once again promised each other that they never repeat their mistakes and always try their best to make each other happy.

At night, they sat on the lawn to plan their trip to Bali. They decided to make this trip memorable for both of them as well.

"How did you get this idea of a trip?" she inquired.

"Hmm... do you want to know?" he asked.

"Yes, that's why I am asking", she replied.

"So, listen, we were so much frustrated with our routine and some other working burden. That's why I decided to take you far away from this work routine. I want to spend more time with you. And not to mention, to refresh our souls by enjoying nature" he replied in a caring way.

"Hmm... pretty impressive Akash!", she said. (They both laughed.)

"Why did you choose Bali?" She asked him again.

"Bali is a breath-taking place. Don't you like it?" he asked her.

"Well, I would go for the Maldives but Bali is fun too. So, no worries, I liked it" she said. "Since you chose this for us" she added more.

(They both went to sleep then.)

Before going to sleep, they both admired each other that they did the right thing and discussed and compromised once again. Not for Suhani but for the Akash it was a milestone. He controlled his temper and worked on the advice given by Rahul. He appreciates that he learned from his life experiences.

He got a random thought what if he gave Anshu another chance to make their relationship strong?

What if I compromised at that time too? No matter what she was my first love. But Akash realized that due to his temper, he lost the most amazing friend of his. His temper is nothing but a pain in the neck.

He once again decided to work more on his temperament and not to hurt people by being so harsh on others.

At the end of the day, he asked himself,

"It is easy to love someone but it is more difficult to be in a relationship. Hence, they are two different things. One doesn't always need compatibility to run a relationship".

CHAPTER ELEVEN

'A TRIP TP BALI'

"Beep Beep, Beep... Beep" The phone vibrated multiple times. Akash was sleeping and his phone was at the side table. Suhani got up due to an annoying phone vibration and she tried to wake Akash to pick up his phone but he was in a deep sleep.

Suhani got the phone from the side table and looked at it. The call was from Shree. She already knew about her but never liked her. Suhani knows that Shree is his sister, but her closeness with Akash always disturbs her. She thought although Akash considers her, his sister, Shree has an interest in him.

She always looks at her suspiciously so she gets skeptical when she sees that Shree calls him late at night.

She was trying to unlock Akash's phone but she didn't even know the password to unlock his phone. She got disturbed and many dubious thoughts were coming to her mind about the phone call.

"Akash never told me that Shree called him late at night", she asked herself in a distrustful way. "She is an irritating girl and she is the one who always disturbs Akash first, and I am sure about it" she answered herself. But she decided to discuss it with Akash and waited for the morning.

The next day, when Akash woke up, he didn't find Suhani next to him. He got worried because it was Sunday and he was off from work as well.

"Where is my phone?" he asked himself while looking for his phone.

He then went downstairs and saw Suhani sitting near the pool. He went to her and asked,

"Hey! What are you doing here? I was looking for you baby girl".

(He sat near her and asked her if she was okay)

He looked at her. She was looking a bit down.

"what's wrong Suhani?", he asked again.

"Who is Shree, Akash?", She directly asked him.

Akash was amazed and simply replied that she was his friend but she was more like a sister to him.

"What's wrong with you Suhani?", he asked.

She looked doubtful and complained to him that why was she calling you late at night. Since Akash was in a deep sleep, he had no idea about his phone as well. He simply said,

"I don't know why was she calling me". He added, "I didn't even check my phone. Where is my phone?"

Suhani gave him his phone and ordered him to call Shree in front of her. Akash was annoyed by her behavior and he confidently called Shree.

"The dialed number is busy at the moment, please try later", the computerized voice said.

Suhani was looking at Akash with her suspicious gloomy eyes. Akash got uncomfortable and asked her what was she thinking about Shree.

"Why are you so insecure about her?" he asked.

Suhani didn't say anything and left the pool sight.

Akash shrugged and felt annoyed. She went back to her in the kitchen and asked her over and over about it.

"Can we talk, please? Akash asked her.

Suhani gazed at him and said nothing. Akash tried to make his position clear and convince her girlfriend that Shree was nothing but a friend. He also said that they used to talk very often. Suhani looked at him again and simply said,

"Call her again".

Akash called Shree again and luckily, she picked up the phone.

"Hey! Akash, how are you? Where are you? I am coming to Bangalore today. Can we meet up brother?" Shree asked him everything without even taking a breath.

Suhani was also listening to her since the phone was on a loudspeaker. She got a bit relaxed when Shree called Akash's Brother.

"Hello Shree, I am fine and living here in Bangalore. When will you arrive here?" Akash asked

"I am already here Akash. Can you please come and pick me up? I need to tell you something about AJ," she requested.

Akash looked at Suhani and she nodded her head and murmured that say yes to her. I want to meet her too.

"Akash? Are you there? Can you come and pick me up? Let me know please", Shree asked her in a hurry.

"Yeah, I am here, and yes. Share your location with me. I and Suhani will come to pick you up," he answered her.

"Okay, check Your WhatsApp. I am sharing my location" she said.

She then disconnected the call and sent Akash her live location.

Akash was looking at Suhani. He was expecting that she would apologize to him for considering him a deceitful person. But she didn't even say anything and went upstairs. Akash was controlling himself because he didn't want to spoil her mood before the trip especially.

Akash got the location of Shree on WhatsApp and asked Suhani to get ready as they had to pick Shree. They then left the house in half an hour.

"What do you think? Why is your friend coming here and wanting to meet you as well?", Suhani inquired.

"Suhani, how would I know this? and she said that she wants to talk about her boyfriend, maybe that's why she wants to meet me." Akash said in a loud voice.

"Boyfriend?" Suhani said shockingly.

"Yes. AJ is her boyfriend. I know him" Akash explained.

"But why didn't you tell me this before?" Suhani said. She looked a bit relaxed now.

"Suhani, when did you ask me about Shree and her relationship? How can I know that you want to know about her?" Akash looked offended.

"No, I mean... she never discussed about him before?" Suhani said.

"Because they are not in any official relationship. Shree didn't want to disclose it yet. They both need some time" Akash explained.

"Right... whatever!" Suhani answers.

Soon, they reached the center mall in Bangalore and picked up Shree from there. Since Akash and Shree had good terms so unconsciously hugged each other as a greeting. Suhani got a bit uncomfortable after looking at them in such a frank manner. They then went back home.

"So, how is life going Shree?", Akash asked her while having dinner.

"Life is so busy these days", she replied while chewing the meal.

"Then what are you doing here in Bangalore? I mean you said that life is so busy", Suhani mocked her while passing her some salad.

"Well, I got so frustrated from my workload that's why I decided to have a trip to Bali", she answered.

"What a coincidence! We are also planning our trip to Bali", Akash exclaimed with surprise.

"Really??? Wow! It would be more fun with you guys on the trip", she exclaimed with excitement.

"But why are you here in Bangalore" Suhani asked her in a dubious voice.

"Oh yeah! My company headquarters is here. I have a one-day work assignment here in the headquarters, that's why I am here ", she replied.

Suhani smiled at her with a smirk and finished her meal.

Akash used to pamper Shree so much because she was like a sister to him. He showed her the guest room as she was tired and wanted to have some rest.

"Please tell me if you need anything," Akash said to Shree.

"Oh yes, you also said that you want to discuss something," Akash asked.

"Yes, but some other time," Shree said hesitatingly. She did so because of Suhani.

Meanwhile, Suhani was not happy with Akash as he was leaning his attention toward his so-called sister. She wasn't talking to Akash as well and was completely down in the dumps.

Akash came closer to Suhani and said,

"Are you still mad at me?"

She was trying to stay away from Akash but Akash grabbed her through her waist and asked her again.

She looked a bit upset and wanted to get the thing off her chest. That's why she asked Akash why didn't he tell her about Shree, adding more to her inquiries she also asked him why was he being so friendly with her. She expressed her feelings once again in front of him and said that she loved him more than anything in the world but sometimes she got insecure because she didn't want to lose the love of his life.

Akash made her comfortable and let her sit on the bed. He explained to her that Shree was more like a sister to him and there was nothing else between them except having a good friendship.

"You don't need to worry about anything, Suhani," he said with a modulated voice.

"Look at me now" he requested her.

When she looked at him, he said romantically,

"I don't want to see tears in those smoky eyes of yours".

She smiled and stopped him from being so romantic all the time. (They both smiled)

The next day, they decided to go shopping. They both invited Shree as well but she had her work in the headquarters.

Suhani and Akash went shopping and bought some necessary stuff for the trip. They both were very happy because it was their first trip as a couple. Before that Akash went there once with his family and he also made some friends there. He was hoping to meet them once again.

They spent all day packing their bags for the trip. Shree also helped them in packing their stuff. They weren't really worried about any guide because Akash knew many of the places there.

Meanwhile, during her stay with Suhani and Akash, Shree was trying to talk to Akash. She was a bit nervous. Akash was like a brother to him that's why she was a bit confused about his response.

"Are you okay Shree? You look a bit low", Akash asked her while she was sitting at the pool sight.

"Yes, I am good" she replied in a low voice.

"Are you sure?", he said. "You know you can tell me, right? Is everything all right between you and AJ?" he added.

"Akash..." she was about to tell her about her relationship problems with Abhay but Suhani came up and asked Akash to help her.

Akash left as Suhani called him.

Shree took a deep breath as she wanted to tell him something but she wasn't able to tell him because of Suhani. She decided to tell Akash about her relationship with AJ in Bali.

The other day, they departed for Bali by air. They were so much excited about their trip. They already had planned a lot of activities to do in Bali. After reaching Bali, they first stayed at the top five-star hotel in Bali. They got two separate rooms. One was for Shree, and the other was for Akash and Suhani.

After resting for a while, they left the hotel for Uluwatu Temple, also known as Pura Luhur.

"Since I know the place very well, I will give you guys a bit of facts and figures about the place," Akash said to both the ladies. According to Akash's knowledge, the Uluwatu is one of the six key temples that are the spiritual pillars of Bali. And perched on top of a cliff approximately 70 meters above sea level. He continued explaining and said,

"The temple is renowned for its magnificent location and is considered to be one of the classic activities in Bali."

Soon after that, they went to the temple sight and were left amazed after seeing the sight.

It was built in a magnificent location. Suhani was a very good photographer. She had a camera with her. She took many pictures at the temple sight.

They also met some travelers there and took pictures with them. Both Suhani and Akash were enjoying the sight and were taking beautiful landscape pictures of the renowned temple. They were so indulged in each other that they forgot about Shree.

Suddenly, Shree went missing, she escaped from the place. Suhani and Akash got worried about her. Akash tried to call her but she wasn't picking up the phone. They both got worried for her.

"Where did she go? Oh, man!! Pick up the phone", asked Akash to himself while calling.

"It's okay Akash, she will be alright," Suhani said.

They looked around the place to find Shree but she was nowhere. Then after half an hour, she appeared out of nowhere. Suhani and Akash asked her where was she.

"I left my bottle in the parking, I went there to get it back," she said innocently.

"Oh Shree, you have no idea, we got so much worried for you," Akash said to Shree holding her by her shoulders.

Suhani again felt that insecurity from Shree but she was pretending to be okay.

Akash took a deep breath and asked both of them to stay with him.

"Please stay close to me. Don't get escaped" Akash overstated.

He further exaggerated, "The place is completely unknown to you people."

(They both nodded.)

It was evening, they enjoyed the place and now felt hungry.

"Let's have something to eat", Shree said.

"Yes, I am hungry too", Suhani replies.

"Okay, Let's move towards the food court. It's nearby within walking distance", Akash suggested. "What do you think guys?", he further asked.

"Okay", they both reply at the same time.

They went to the food court.

"Akash! Have you tried Bali's traditional food? I've heard a lot about it", Suhani asked.

"Yes, I tried it some two years ago when I came here with my family", Akash replies.

"Nasi Goreng" Shree interrupted both of them.

"How do you know that Shree?", Akash asked.

Shree laughed and said,

"I have some friends here in Bali, Akash"

Akash raised his eyebrows with wonder and said with a smirk,

"Your Friends?"

They both then laugh. But things were quite irritating for Suhani because she never knew about their bond. She was just trying to swallow this bitterness of the moment because she seemed so insecure about Shree and Akash's bond of attachment.

Her insecurity was natural because she loved Akash more than anything else not to mention. Girls get uncomfortable when their boys show even a little bit of a caring attitude toward other females. She tried to accept the reality told by Akash, but Shree wasn't his sister by blood relationship.

Her insecurities were quite authentic.

After having the Bali cuisine, they went back to their hotels. Suhani was so tired that they went to sleep and Shree also went to her room for some rest. Akash was not that much tired and didn't want to rest. He decided to read a book. This time he brought many interesting books to read.

He opened up his bag pack and brought out all of the two books. Since he started reading Forty Rules of Love back then in Bangalore, he decided to continue reading the book. He continued reading until he read a line,

"I slept peacefully that night, feeling exultant and determined. Little did I know that I was making the most common and most painful mistake women have made throughout the ages: to naively think that with their love they can change the man they love"

(He sighs after reading this line)

He was sitting on the balcony and went into deep thoughts. He got hurt by Suhani's attitude and was annoyed by her stupid unwanted argument. This particular line made him realize if a woman can't be able to change a man with her love, then how a man would be able to do the same thing?

He thought to himself, "Perfect love story doesn't exist".

He was looking out of the balcony when he saw Shree sitting at the pool sight. He then remembered that a day before their departure to Bali, Shree was about to share something with him.

He went inside the room and looked at Suhani. She was in a deep sleep. Akash thought that I should accompany Shree since she was also here to enjoy. He opened the door and went to the pool sight to accompany Shree.

Shree was preoccupied with her thoughts when Akash came to interrupt her.

"Hi," Akash addressed her.

She turned around her face to find out that someone was calling her and it was Akash. She responded with a smile.

Akash came near to her and inquired,

"What are you doing here my beautiful sister? Don't you tire?"

"No, I am good", Shree replies.

Akash said that if she wanted to share anything with him, he was always here to talk and to listen.

"Can I ask something Akash?", her voice was low.

"Of course," Akash assured her.

"Are you happy with Suhani?", she asked Akash.

(Akash sighed)

"Honestly speaking, I don't know," I am also trying to figure out this" Akash said in a depressed way.

"I am having a tough time with AJ", Shree boldly told him.

She then told him about AJ and how they used to fight over every little thing.

"Maybe it's just a tough time. Have you talked to him about all this?" Akash asked.

"Yes, I always try to make things better, but..." Shree starts crying.

"Hey, please Shree... Stop. You are a strong girl. Please don't worry." Akash said. He looked worried for her.

"We will talk about it later... you need to sleep now" Akash advised.

They said goodnight to each other and went to sleep.

The next day, they had to visit the most beautiful part of the trip. It was Bali Swing. Suhani was so excited about the swing since it was the most amazing and worthy sight of their trip. They got up and left the Hotel after having their breakfast.

"You look beautiful", Akash admired Suhani.

"Thank You", Suhani replies.

"Where did you get this eye-catching beauty?" Akash tried to express his feelings about her beauty.

"We are getting late, Let's go now", Suhani ignored his question and went outside the room. Shree was standing outside their room. They all then went outside.

"Akash?" Suhani called him.

"Hmm...?" Akash replied in a low tone.

"Where did your guide version go? Won't you tell us today about Bali swing?" Suhani mocked him.

(Akash laughed)

"Umm... I never went to Bali swing, that's I guess a place for females not for males", Akash replies.

The driver interrupted them and asked to help them as a guide to Bali Swing. They allowed him to guide them since all of them were unaware of that place.

The guide then told them that they could visit Tegalalang Rice Terrace and Sacred Monkey Forest Sanctuary as well because these were the most nearby places to Bali Swing. He also exaggerated that the best way to admire the rice terrace of Bali is through Bali swing.

Now Suhani was so excited because she was already in love with the natural environment of Bali and couldn't wait to take a ride on a Bali swing.

When they reached their final destination, they were completely lost in their thought about the beautiful and breathtaking view of Bali. Suhani went to the Swing side and took pictures. Luckily, she got a friend there from high school and they got so happy to see each other after a while.

His friend had come there with a group of travelers and he also served as a group guide. He knew the whole mystery of the Bali swing. He told them that from rope swings that take us further into the aesthetic wilderness of Bali to a range of tours that will appeal to the adventurer in us.

He further said, "The theme park in Abiansemal is popular for its endearing welcome and fun activities".

Then they both got busy talking and Akash remained alone with Shree.

"Why are you so worried?" Shree asked.

"Shree? Why all the relationships are so hard? Why everyone is in so much pain? Why do we always have to pretend that we are happy?" Akash said.

"What makes you think like that?" Shree asked. She saw pain in his eyes. He could have been anything at that time, but he was not happy.

"I used to think, that I am the only one who is suffering continuously... but after listening about you and AJ, I am shocked, and disappointed" Akash explained.

"We will try to figure out the solution. Come with me" Shree said.

Since Suhani was busy with her tour guide friend they both went to the nearby sitting area. Shree explained everything about her relationship with AJ to Akash.

"We are so close to each other. We don't want to leave each other side but apart from our love for each other, we still have so many differences and recently these differences have led us to a severe fight", she explained with sorrow. She further said, "A relationship requires a firm credence from both parties".

Akash was getting Shree's point because he was also facing these things in his relationship with Suhani.

"Last night, you asked me about my position in my relationship with Suhani"

Akash recalled Shree's question.

"Yes! Because I want you to tell me how can I manage these differences just for the sake of our love", Shree said to Akash in a teary voice.

"You are right Shree. Apart from everything, firm belief and trust are the most important components of a relationship and we all lack this credence in our relationships", Akash averred this reality to Shree.

"Are we on the same page?", Shree asked Akash with worry.

"Yes, Shree! We both are suffering from the same thing. " Akash said.

"Akash, I came to Bangalore just for this reason because I wanted to talk to you. I needed you so badly back then. I wanted to tell you, my problem. I believe that you are experienced in this relationship stuff so you could tell me what the right thing to do is", Shree explained.

"I am sorry, I didn't get the time to talk to you because I got so much busy with my work and personal life", Akash apologized.

They both had a long conversation about their relationships. Akash also explained everything to her about their recent fight. They both were completely in a state of distress.

"I can't compromise it when it comes to my personal space" Shree continued to explain.

"Personal space is a part of a relationship. One needs to compromise for it because other than that a relationship will never last ", Akash said to Shree.

"I and Suhani had so many fights but we chose to compromise every time. But sometimes it makes me so annoying when she overrated over a small issue. A relationship doesn't mean that two people are bound to get permission from each other before going to do anything" he explained.

"I am sick of it because I have to bend the knee every time," he said in a cacophony.

"Our relationship has become nothing except a blame game. We do nothing except ranting each other all the time", Shree said with apathy.

Meanwhile, they were talking, and Suhani came back to hand over Akash's mobile to him. She also informed him that his phone was ringing continuously. He unlocked his phone to check the call history. It was Rahul and he tried to call him back but his number was busy at that moment. Suddenly, a notification appeared that completely shattered him into pieces. He looked at Shree with tears.

"We need to get back home", Akash said in a hurry with teary eyes and went to Suhani to tell her about their urgent return.

Shree ran after Akash.

CHAPTER TWELVE

'A TOPSY-TURVY RELATIONSHIP'

"Mom please, just one more bite", Akash requested his mother.

"No Akash, I don't want to eat it anymore, you know I never like cereals", his mother insisted him not to force her anymore.

"But Mom doctors have recommended it for you since you can't eat any heavy dietary food now", he tried to convince his mother.

"Ugh... Okay but only one more bite", her mother groaned.

They were in the hospital. Akash was helping his mom get better since she had her heart surgery a week before. He was trying his best to give all the attention to his mother. He wasn't attending the office in Bangalore but he was working from home in Delhi. He truly understood the condition of his mother that's why he returned to Delhi. The old age of his parents made him realize that they needed him. He was ashamed that he didn't even know that his beloved mother was a heart patient. He was so guilty and repented for being a careless son.

They heard the sound of footsteps towards them when he was attending to his mother. It was Rahul, who came with a bouquet.

"Hello! My beautiful aunt", Rahul addressed Akash's mom.

"Hey! Rahul, I was just waiting for you", Akash rushed towards him and they hugged.

Rahul came to see Akash's mother since they guys were childhood friends that's why his mother means a lot to Rahul as well. He came with so many fruits and healthy food with him as hospitality. He comforted Akash's mom that now his two sons had come, she didn't need to worry anymore. Akash's mother was a bit more relaxed when Rahul came to visit her. They talked for a while.

"Okay Mom, Doctor said that you are not allowed to talk this much, now get some rest. We are staying outside", Akash said to her mother.

"Yes! We will be there to get you some medicine. Now you have to take a nap as well", Rahul said to Akash's mother.

(They left the room)

They walked through the corridor and went to the cafeteria. They ordered something to eat. While they were waiting for their meal. Rahul tried to talk to Akash.

"Well, perhaps this whole situation ruined your trip but how's Bali anyway?" Rahul asked Akash.

"It was just like before. You know we have already visited that place some years back", Akash replied in a frustrated way.

"But this time, you went there with the person you love. It must be more beautiful this time", Rahul said.

"Ah! The person I love", Akash said in a frustrated way.

"Hmm... why didn't she come with you?" Rahul asked.

The waiter served their meal and Akash ignored Rahul's question. Akash had started eating his meal.

"I mean, she should be with you at this time of hour", Rahul added.

"I don't want to talk about her Rahul", Akash emphasized.

(Rahul shrugged)

Rahul also had started eating his meal. He had an idea about their relationship that's why he didn't force Akash. He knew that he would come to him at the end of the day with his problem. He tried to engage him in something else. He told him about his newly launched office in Delhi. Akash appreciated that he had actually achieved his goal.

"You always wanted to have your own company", Akash said

"Yes, and you know I worked so hard to achieve my goal", Rahul replies.

"East, west, south, or north makes little difference. No matter what your destination, just be sure to make every journey a journey within. If you travel within, you'll travel the whole wide world and beyond".

Akash recalled a line from his favorite book, Forty Rules of Love.

"Oh! Wow, I remember this rule, it's rule 9. Right?" Rahul acknowledged Akash.

"Have you read it?", Akash asked.

"Of course, you recommended me this book and I loved it", Rahul replied with joy.

"Thank God, finally you read something recommended by me", Akash mocked him.

(They laughed)

Rahul finally was able to engage Akash in something else than a relationship. They talked about business, selling, and marketing as well. They also suggested each other to work together in their home city. Rahul also told him that he was going to stay with Akash here in the hospital. And that's what friends do.

"You are the only person that understands me", said Akash to Rahul.

Rahul smiled and said, "And you can always count on me".

(Akash sighed)

He told himself that his love story was nothing but a sailing boat and maybe he hadn't found a perfect love yet but at least he was already given with a perfect friend.

While they were having their meal, Akash's father called him. He attended the call and his father informed him on the call that his mother needed him. They both left the food in the middle and went to the cardiology department. Akash's heart was beating so fast. When he went to her mother's room, he saw that his father was crying so much. He almost lost his senses when he approached his mother's bed.

But when he saw his mother's face which almost turned pale at that time, he got fainted. Rahul ran to hold Akash as he had lost his senses. It was a terrible moment. His father was also crying as he had lost the love of his life. Now Akash was the only support to his father after his mother. The whole moment was nothing but torment for all of them.

Akash's phone rang. But he fainted because of the severe shock he just got a few minutes ago. Rahul was the only one in the room to manage the situation. He ignored the call in the first place and called the nurse for help. He cried with pain,

"Please, someone help us".

The doctor and the nurses came inside and got panicked after seeing the view.

"Hurry up nurse, take them to the emergency", doctors commanded. They took Akash to the emergency through a stretcher. They also got something for Akash's father. Rahul called his other friends and acknowledged them with this torment of hell. He called some of Akash's relatives as well to inform them about the death of Akash's mother and their current situation in the hospital. Akash's phone was constantly ringing. Rahul got his phone out of his pocket and he saw that there were 11 miscalls on his phone.

On the other hand, Shree was constantly calling Akash. She wanted to know about Akash's mother's health. During their return flight from Bali, Akash told her about her mother's heart attack news. That's why she wanted to know about their situation.

He picked up the phone and answered it.

It's Shree, "Akash! How are you? How's your mother now? ", Shree said in a low voice.

"I am sorry...", Rahul replied in a teary voice.

"Excuse me?", Shree said.

"Shree... it's me Rahul", Rahul replies.

"Oh! Rahul, how are you? where is Akash?", Shree asked.

"Akash has been shifted to the emergency ward since he got fainted", Rahul replies.

"What? But why? Is everything okay there? ", She asked in a worry.

"Actually...", Rahul was trying to tell her the truth.

"His mother passed away", he said without taking a breath.

"What?", Shree replied loudly.

Rahul was also in pain so he disconnected the call. He went to Akash in the emergency ward.

Akash didn't come back to his senses at that time. Rahul was so much worried about his best friend. Shree again called Akash's phone and this time it was picked up by Rahul again.

"Can you please share Akash's location with me? I am coming to Delhi to visit Akash", Shree said without taking a breath.

Rahul replied, "I'll send you the location right away".

Shree disconnected the call. Rahul went to Akash; he didn't get up till then. His concerns were aggrandizing gradually. He went to Akash's father and tried to help him in putting himself. The doctors came to Rahul in the middle of the situation as they wanted to discharge the dead body from the occupied room. Rahul got busy handling the paperwork. Meanwhile, Shree reminded him again to send the location. Rahul then sent the location to Shree.

In the evening a nurse came to Rahul, "Excuse me sir?", the nurse addressed Rahul.

Rahul was sitting in the waiting area when a nurse came to him to tell him about Akash. "Yes", Rahul replies.

"Your friend has just got up, and he is looking for someone", the nurse told him.

Rahul went to Akash in a minute. He approached his bed and hugged him so tightly. He looked at Rahul then and tried to comfort him.

"I never knew that. It can't happen. I can't lose my mom. God can't be this cruel Rahul", Akash said while he was sobbing.

"It's okay Akash. God knows better", he tried to convince him that he had to accept the reality.

"I didn't even get a chance to talk to her in the last moments of her departure", Akash complained himself.

Rahul was in tears and tried to control himself because he was the only one to help Akash at that moment.

Communicating with somebody who is miserable and hurting can be awkward; you want to be around for them, express your empathy, and develop your bond, but you don't know how to act or what to say. Rahul was in the same position. He wanted to console him but his heart was also in pain.

Suddenly, Akash's phone rang. It was Shree, she wanted to talk to Akash and wanted to tell him that she was there for him. Akash picked up her phone and started crying. Shree got more upset and tried to solace him. He told her in pain that his mother passed away. Shree told him that she was at Delhi airport and coming to his home directly. Akash disconnected the call.

"We have to go home now Akash", said Rahul.

Akash looked at him, he didn't consider himself ready for this.

"I can't do this Rahul", he cried.

"But you have to. I know you are in pain and it is very hard time for you. I know that you are hurting, but you also have to console your father Akash", Rahul emphasized.

He further added, "Your father needs you, Akash. Many of your relatives are also outside with your father but he needs you".

Her mother's death left them in torment. Now it was time to take the dead body to the house. The moment they lifted his mother's body, he once again crashed to the ground in agony. Rahul gave him some courage to swallow this bitter reality.

On the other hand, Shree tried to call Suhani. She was still in Bangalore. But she knew that she would never pick up her phone.

Shree had flashbacks of the whole scenario when Akash and Suhani got into a severe argument just because of her. She didn't even ask Akash about his mother's health. Actually, she fought with him in a fury, and the reason was the urgent return from Bali.

That's why she didn't go to Delhi with Akash. But Shree didn't bother this at all and she called her again. She didn't answer her. But when Shree left a text to her about the death of Akash's mother, she called Shree back immediately.

"I am sorry, I just checked my phone right now", Suhani said.

"Akash's mother had passed away Suhani", Shree said in a low voice,

"I just read your message. I am sorry for her. May God rest her soul in peace", Suhani said.

"Will you come to Delhi?", Shree asked.

"Of course, I am already guilty for my actions. Apart from everything, I should be more concerned for her mother" " she said in a remorseful way.

"I am in Delhi. I am now heading towards his home", Shree informed her.

"Okay, please inform me about Akash. I'll try to come there as soon as I can", Suhani said.

"Please come soon Suhani, you have no idea how much he loves you", Shree said.

"Hmm...", Suhani murmured.

"I want to see both of you happy. Don't take our relationship wrong. For me Akash is just like a brother", Shree said. She further added, "I'll send you his residential address. Please come, Akash needs your support now. He has suffered from anguish".

"Okay, I'll be there soon. Stay in contact with me", Suhani said and disconnected the call.

Suhani was feeling so guilty. She knew that her foolishness would ruin would relationship someday. She was now at that moment realizing that she had made a big mistake. She can imagine that losing a mother was more painful than anything else.

"It shouldn't be like that", she said to herself. "I always wanted to be a dominant one in the relationship. I didn't realize that it was Akash who was working for this relationship and making all the compromises without letting me know", She was accusing herself.

She was now thinking about Akash all the time. She also knew that she and Akash had many differences but she didn't want to lose Akash. She was so much baffled about their relationship now. She was about to call him, but then she stopped. She packed up her necessities and booked a ticket for Delhi.

She thought "Greif is like the ocean; it comes in waves ebbing and flowing. Sometimes the water is calm, and sometimes it is overwhelming. All we can do is learn to swim".

She could imagine that Akash was in pain but he had to accept the reality. She wanted to go to him right away but she never got an urgent flight to Delhi. She then booked the ticket to Delhi for the next date.

In Delhi, Akash had already spent a day without his mother.

All the family and friends had visited the home of the bereaved to offer their sympathy. All the necessary traditional customs were also done. Shree and Rahul both were on the front line in handling the whole situation. Akash locked himself in his room and cried for the rest of the day. At night, the last person that came to Akash's home was Suhani. Rahul welcomed her into the home.

She then met Shree and was sorry that she wasn't able to come on time. Rahul knocked on Akash's room and informed him about the arrival of Suhani. Akash was in pain and didn't want to be part of another argument with Suhani. The primary cause of his pain was his mother's death, but the anguish he was within was because of Suhani.

He gave her everything. Instead of ending, he tried to keep up his relationship with Suhani, but the past few days had made him realize that they had so many differences and a relationship never works with hundreds of differences.

We all have dreams, goals, and expectations when we start a relationship. But what happens if a promise isn't kept? What happens if things don't turn out the way we planned? A person shatters!

And it has become a shattering experience for Akash.

"I don't want to meet anyone", he said.

"Akash! It's Suhani", Rahul repeated.

"I don't care anymore", Akash said.

"Akash!", Rahul said.

"Tell her, that it was only one person who truly loved him and it was her mother and now she has gone", he cried.

Rahul went back downstairs and told both Shree and Suhani that Akash didn't want to meet anyone. Shree tried to handle the situation and took Suhani to the guest room.

"You must be tired, Let's go. Get some rest now", Shree said.

"I want to see him", she emphasized.

Rahul and Shree looked at each other. Shree took her to Akash's room and went back downstairs.

"Akash?", Suhani mournfully called him.

"Please, open the door and talk to me", she further said.

Akash opened the door in anger. He almost lost his temper and he cried with anger,

"Why are you here now?"

His voice was so loud that Rahul and Shree went upstairs right away.

"I don't want to be with you anymore Suhani. You snatched everything from me. I can't be with such a selfish person at all", he cried.

"I know Akash. I can't understand your situation. But I am here to apologize. Please calm down", Suhani's voice was trembling while convincing him.

"Go away Suhani, you are such a selfish person", Akash overrated.

"Suhani please come with me. It's not the right time", Shree advised and took Suhani with her to the guest room.

Rahul also tried to calm down Akash and offered him a glass of water. He was in fury and tore the glass into pieces. Rahul groaned at Akash. But he didn't leave his side and he calmed down Akash. After a while, Akash calmed down a bit.

"You still don't have control over your temper", Rahul said.

"I don't know. I can't change myself for anyone", he replied.

"Akash she is here to talk to you. Please don't do this to her. Give her a chance", Rahul advised him.

"I don't want anything right now", Akash said.

Shree came and told them that Suhani was crying so hard and wanted to go home. Rahul looked at Akash and fell to his knees.

"Akash talk to her, my boy! Clear everything", he emphasized.

Shree also said the same thing to Akash.

Since both of them emphasized him a lot so, he got convinced and went to her. She was walking on the lawn.

"I am sorry. I lost my temper", Akash said to her with guilt.

"You were right. You lost your temper. And I... I lost you as well. I am sorry Akash. I am not the right person for you" " she said with regret.

"Look Suhani, we have so many differences and you can't deny it", Akash said.

"I know and I am not denying anything", she replied.

They both realized that these differences were not easy to tackle now. They were not able to compromise all the time. That night they both lost each other but Akash was the one who lost the most.

People bring different perspectives, talents, and strengths to a relationship. You might appreciate some of the things your partner has to offer – great cooking, their sense of humor, good sex, getting on well with your family and friends – but you might not like their taste in music, the time they spend on technology, or the fact they get stressed easily. Some conflict in relationships is inevitable, but there are ways to handle it so it is not destructive to you individually or as a couple", Suhani explained.

Akash wasn't ready to ameliorate this time. He wanted to have some time.

"I can't leave my father alone now", Akash said.

"I understand", she replied.

"Our differences are not normal Suhani. One can't compromise for his/her personal space in a relationship. There are so many other things that we have to take care of while having a relationship", Akash complained.

"Do you really want to end this?", she asked.

"You made so many things so overrated that I can't forget them. You blamed me for nothing. You didn't even try to build that credence in our relationship. You got insecure with Shree. You don't want me to stay outside with my friends", he explained with agony.

"Why did you hide all the things from me? You should tell me about my mistakes at that moment" she replied.

"I wanted you to realize yourself but you tore my confidence in you into pieces when you chose to stay in Bangalore and wasn't ready to come with me to Delhi for my mother", he complained again.

"This is nothing but a topsy-turvy relationship, and we can't make it work like this," he further emphasized.

"Go and live your way from now. I can't continue a relationship that has so many differences and no credence", he said and went inside the house.

The fear she had in her heart came true. Akash's last words tore her at that moment.

CHAPTER THIRTEEN

'LOVE IS AN ILLUSION'

"Mr. Akash! Your appointment has been delayed due to an emergency", the consultant of the therapist informed Akash.

He went back to his home with Shree. Akash and his father were the only people left in their home so Rahul and Shree decided to live with them. The main reason behind it was Akash's mental health. They both wanted to get back the Akash they had in the first place.

"Hmm... this smell!", Shree said.

(Akash didn't respond)

"Akash?", She poked him

"Yes", he replied unconsciously.

"We are home", she said with a smirk on her face.

(They got out of the car and walked towards the lawn)

His father was waiting for him at lunch. His father had always been a good cook.

He cooked Akash's favorite sandwich; a double cheese chicken sandwich. They went to the lawn and enjoyed lunch. They all were trying to get back to normal. Ostensibly, they were still unable to forget the tragedy of their beloved only female family member, even after six months. Due to Akash's unwanted temperament problems, Rahul and Shree decided to take him to the therapist.

"Did you visit the therapist?", Rahul asked Akash.

"No", Akash replied.

"We went to the clinic but the appointment was delayed", Shree replied to Rahul.

Akash left them all on the lawn and went inside his room. He usually spent all day in the room. Shree and Rahul tried to engage him in different activities but he made up his mind not to do anything. Apart from all of this, he spent most of his time reading books. He had already completed many books. But his super favorite was still Forty Rules of Love.

The doldrums took him to spend most of his time thinking about his mistakes in the past. He regrated for so many things. And this melancholy was not helping me out to move on.

Shree knocked on the door and came inside.

"Hi! I loved this book. I am here to return it to you. Here you go", said Shree in a thankful way.

"Who recommended you this book to?", Akash asked

He further guessed, " Your boyfriend?"

She laughed.

"No, it was recommended by your friend, Rahul", she replied.

"What about AJ?", He asked.

She sighed

"It's been half a year, we didn't talk", she replied.

"Why?", He asked.

"I left my job and he left India", she said.

"Hmm... Did you give him a chance?", He asked with curiosity.

"My love wasn't enough for him, I guess. And my love wasn't that powerful to stop him from leaving India", she replied.

"Did you give him a chance?", He asked again.

"What else did he want from me? I left my family for him. My family wasn't ready to accept my relationship with AJ. But for the sake of my life, I left them all. And was ready to stay with him and to support him through every thick and thin", she explained.

"Then he didn't love you I guess", he said.

"Love is nothing but a mystery," she said

"Wrong!", He neglected her statement and said,

"Love is nothing but an illusion".

They looked at each other and Shree went back to Rahul.

Akash locked up his room and once again cried so much. He was so much disappointed with the person he loved in his life. First Anshu and then Suhani left him in a period of stagnation.

He lost his first love because it was part of the teenage era, and usually, people made silly mistakes at that age. But his love for Suhani was so pure. Unfortunately, he can't forget those beautiful days of his relationship with Suhani. Whenever he thought about the happy memories, the unwanted bad memories replaced and ruined the moment.

At night, they all decided to go for dinner outside. Akash's father was invited to a dinner arranged by his friends so he went there already. Shree and Rahul took Akash to the most beautiful rooftop of Delhi. They decided to have some activities there.

"What will you eat Shree?", Rahul asked Shree.

"Stuffed chicken", she replied.

"And what about you Akash?", He asked Akash

"I'll go with the salad only", he replied.

(They both looked at Akash because they knew that Akash didn't like vegetables)

wait! Are you on a diet?" Rahul asked with surprise.

"No", he replied.

" But you don't like vegetables", Shree added.

"But I want to eat it as well", he replied.

(They both were looking at him with astonishment)

The moment they swallowed the peculiar desire of Akash, they ordered the food for dinner.

"Salad?", Rahul asked once again.

Akash gave a serious look to Rahul

"Okay, Chill boy", Rahul replied.

"Everyone thinks of changing the world, but no one thinks of changing himself.", Akash quoted.

"Can I ask a question?", Shree said.

Akash looked at Shree and nodded.

"Did you know that your mother was a heart patient?", Shree added.

Rahul coughed after hearing the Shree question

"No", Akash said.

Shree was about to ask further. But Rahul interrupted her in the middle of the way. He suggested playing a game. He didn't want to remind Akash about his family issues. Rahul knew everything about Akash and his family. He didn't want Akash to tell Shree anything especially not right there during the dinner.

Akash said, "What kind of game?".

Rahul suggested playing "Antakshri".

"No, no, no! Not Antakshri, I am not a good singer at all", Shree rejected the idea.

Rahul said, "We are not going to give anyone a tag of good singer here. Just sing and play".

Akash said, " Yes, no judgments"

They started playing Antakshri. It was a well-known hotel, and many people were already there that's why there was some time in their dinner to be served.

"Only English songs are allowed in this music play", Rahul said.

"Wait! Why English?", Akash asked.

"Because we know that you don't listen to Hindi songs", Rahul replied.

"That doesn't matter. Let's prioritize Hindi songs", Akash said.

They both were astonished once again because they noticed that Akash was trying to challenge many different things. Especially the ones he never liked or loved in his past.

"Okay, cool!", Rahul said.

They then played the game and had a lot of fun. They were mainly laughing over their voices. Meanwhile, Akash is lost in the memories of his past. He unconsciously told them that Suhani used to listen to so many Hindi songs that's why he was also a bit aware of them. But when he noticed what he said, he looked at Shree and Rahul and tried to distract them again.

"It's now your turn, Shree", he passed the last word of the song.

Meanwhile, their dinner had arrived. The waiter served Akash with the salad.

Rahul said, "I guess Suhani also motivated you for the vegetables as well".

(Akash smiled)

He once again said unconsciously,

"Of course, she loved vegetable salads".

The situation became more complicated for him because he hadn't even talked to her in the past six months. It was clear from his face and thoughts that he was missing her so much worse. Rahul overcame the situation and asked them to eat hurry because they had to watch the movie as well.

"Shree, guess what", Rahul asked Shree.

"What?", Shree replied.

"I got us some tickets for the End Game", Rahul said with excitement.

" Damn... I love the Marvel Series", She replied.

"Yes, we all do", Rahul said.

Akash noticed that Rahul looked a bit interested in Shree. He was happy because he trusted Rahul more than anything and Shree was already like her sister. He thought that he would ask Rahul first about his feelings for Shree.

"Okay, let's go home", Rahul said.

Shree's phone rang.

"Oh, it's my mother", she picked up the phone.

They were leaving the rooftop. They had to go back to Akash's home since they all lived there. But Shree then came and informed them that she had to go back home urgently.

"Is everything okay?", They both asked Shree.

"Yes, all good", she replied. "My mother is missing me. I haven't seen her for the last two months" she explained.

"Oh! Do you want me to take you home?" Rahul said.

Akash was smiling and now he was confirmed that Rahul liked her. Rahul noticed it when Akash was smiling.

"No, it's okay. My driver is coming to pick me up", she said.

"Hmm... Okay good", Rahul replied.

They left the hotel when Shree's driver arrived.

Akash and Rahul were going back home when Akash looked at him with curiosity. Rahul was driving.

"You know you can share with me anything", Akash said.

Rahul gave him a look and spoke.

"Yes, I know".

"Talk to her, Rahul", Akash said.

"Talk to whom?", He replied.

"I am not a blind person, and I can clearly see your feelings for Shree", He said.

"Oh! Really?" He spoke.

"Now tell me the truth", Akash emphasized.

"There is nothing like that bro", Rahul replied.

"You know, I can tell you by looking at your face that you are lying", Akash said.

(Rahul murmured)

Rahul liked her but he didn't want to ruin the beautiful relationship they already had. He had a fear of losing her as a friend because she already had suffered a lot.

"What if she got angry?" Rahul said to himself and he was continuously thinking about her when they were on their way.

They reached home. The guard opened the door and Rahul parked the car. They got out of the car. Rahul was trying not to look at Akash. He went inside the house. Akash went back to him because he wanted to know the truth. He wanted Rahul to express his feelings for Shree.

"Rahul, Rahul, Rahul, listen!", He called Rahul. Rahul looked back at him and said,

"Hmm...? " He replied.

"Rahul, tell me the truth. You know that you can count on me. I am Akash, your best friend. More than a brother to you", he emphasized.

"I am sitting on the fence", Rahul replied.

"But why?", Akash asked.

"Because... Because I don't know what to do", he said in a frustrated way.

Akash took him to his room and calmed him down.

"I am afraid of being rejected by someone Akash. I also had feelings for my school classmate but she had rejected me. I don't want to be rejected by someone again", he said with disappointment.

"Rejection is a new opportunity, Rahul," Akash said thoughtfully. He further said,

"You are a perfect man, brother! You don't need to think about such a stupid thing. Just go and let her know about your feelings. Don't be afraid of rejection".

"But you were too in a relationship, you were so happy, and suddenly, due to having differences, your relationship went down the flames", said Rahul.

"I have missed the bullet. Suhani is a perfect woman. Just because of my temperament, I lost that opportunity of such an amazing life partner", Akash regrated.

(Rahul shrugged his shoulder)

"I've learned now, that mutual differences are just like that drop in the ocean. At that moment if I was at her place, I'd definitely do the same thing", Akash said.

"She was a good catch for you", Rahul said.

"But my temperament had driven her up to a wall. She will not talk to me now. She doesn't even think of me after all of that", Akash said.

Rahul said, "Go and talk to her".

Rahul looked at Akash and said he would see that later. He emphasized Rahul's talk to Shree. He also advised him, not to miss the bullet now.

Rahul took a deep breath, and rest assured that he had decided to talk with Shree. Akash was a bit relaxed now.

The next day, Akash called Shree and asked her about her arrival back to Delhi. She informed him that she would be there tomorrow. Akash was excited and waiting anxiously for Shree. He also informed Rahul that Shree would be there tomorrow. Rahul got nervous.

"It's so hard", Rahul said in a trembling voice.

Akash laughed and said, "It isn't".

"What will you say to her? ", Akash asked.

"I don't know", Rahul said.

"Let's practice!" Akash emphasized

"No, please do not put me in such a weird position", Rahul requested.

"But at least tell me, what will you say to her", Akash asked.

They both got busy planning the proposal. Akash told him that Shree was an introverted woman. Rahul got more nervous. Akash gave him a couple of ideas for the proposal. He also advised him,

"If someone seriously wants to be a part of your life, they will seriously make an effort to be in it. No reason. No excuse".

"She is a generous woman. I will never force her to be a part of my life", Rahul said.

Akash spanked on his back and gave him some courage.

"Just remember my advice", Akash said and left the house.

The next day Akash and Rahul were having a cup of tea on a lawn. They were chit-chatting. Akash was teasing Rahul. They were about to leave the lawn when they saw Shree coming to them.

"Hello beautiful humans!", Shree said.

Rahul got nervous when he saw her coming to them. He was whispering not to say anything about his feelings.

"Hi, Shree", Akash replied.

They greeted and spent more time on the lawn. Suddenly, Shree remembered that she got something for

Rahul and Akash.

"I got something for you," she said with excitement.

"What is it?", Akash asked.

She gave them two boxes of gifts. "I bought these for you from Agra", she said.

Akash opened up his gift and got a sculpture of The Thinker, Auguste Rodin.

Akash already had so many sculptures. She got him something for him that manifests his nature.

"Wow, I loved it, Shree". "Thank you so much", he said.

Rahul unwrapped the gift box and got a decorative marble Taj Mahal. He was very happy about this beautiful gift. Akash had that smirk on his face and he mocked Akash.

"Ahan! What a romantic gift", he exclaimed.

Shree looked a bit embarrassed. She justified, " I bought these gifts according to your aesthetic sense. Rahul has a calm nature and he also speaks so politely".

"I was kidding", Akash said.

They both thanked Shree for giving such amazing gifts to them.

They all went inside the house. Shree was tired. She went for some rest after meeting Akash's father.

In the evening, Akash had to go with his father to the doctor. He wished good luck to Rahul and left. Rahul assures him that that he will talk to Shree after Akash leaves the house.

Shree was walking on the lawn. Rahul pulled up his socks and went to the lawn.

"Can I join you?", He asked.

"Yeah, of course", she replied.

"Thank you for the gift by the way", he said.

She smiled.

Suddenly, a brilliant idea crossed his mind and he asked, "Coffee?"

"Of course,", she replied.

"Okay, let's go", he said with excitement.

"Wait! I thought you are going to make it on were own", she said.

He laughed.

"Is it okay if we go out for coffee?" He asked

"Yes, sure", she replied.

"But without Akash?", She asked

"He will get late tonight. Don't worry we will be home before them", he convinced her.

"Okay, let's go then", she said.

They both went to the nearby cafe for coffee. Coincidentally, they both liked cappuccino. They ordered the same thing and tried to engage themselves in a conversation.

"Shree", Rahul said.

"Hmm...?", She replied.

"I wanted to talk to you about something very important thing", he said.

"Go on, I am listening to you", she replied.

"It's hard to explain. But promise me first that you'll not get mad at me", he said in a low voice.

"Stop beating around the bush Rahul, just ask it", she said.

"Shree, I like you so much", he said.

(She didn't say anything and there was complete silence for a while)

"I am sorry. Please don't get mad at me. I didn't want to tell you but I can't hide this from you. I am not forcing you to answer me. I am just... I am just telling you. You are free to make up your mind", he said out of breath.

Shree wasn't mad at him. She was confused because she didn't want to involve herself in a relationship.

"I can't be in a relationship again, Rahul", she replied.

"It's okay", Rahul replied.

"My parents are already looking for someone. They want me to marry as soon as possible. I am their lone child", she explained.

Rahul didn't say anything. They finished their coffee and went back home. On the other hand, Akash was in a hurry to get back home. He wanted to know whether they talked or not. He was curious and wanted to know about Shree's response.

At night, Akash went to Rahul's room straight.

"What did she say?", Akash asked

"Nothing", he replied

"Nothing? Not a single word?", Akash said.

"She said that her parents were already finding someone for her", He told Akash in a low voice.

Akash laughed.

"Why are you laughing?", Rahul looked at him with a serious look and complained.

"Stupid! She gave you a hint", Akash said

"A hint?", Rahul asked with curiosity

"Yes, if she doesn't want to be in a relationship it means that she wanted you to talk to her parents. Or at least send you a proposal to them", Akash explained

"Hmm... Are you sure?", he replied

"Of course, I am", Akash said

Akash's statement left Rahul in deep thoughts once again. Akash left the room to talk to Shree. He went to Shree's room and knocked.

"Shree? Are you up?", he asked.

Shree opened the door. "Yes, I am up. Come in", Shree said.

"You look happy", he asked.

"Stop it. I know that you know everything", she said

Akash laughed.

"Yes, I do", Akash said.

"Tell your friend to send a proposal to my parents", she emphasized.

Akash laughed. He explained to her that Rahul was sitting in the doldrums because of your response. Shree told Akash that she gave him a big hint but he didn't get that. They were both talking about it. Akash was so happy for her close friends.

"You are so dear to me Shree. And believe me, Rahul is a good catch", Akash told her

"I know, I like him as well. He is more sensible and mature. We will be able to have a perfect relationship", she said.

"No relationship is perfect. No one is perfect in this world. If we want to have a long and ever-lasting relationship, we have to build that mutual understanding first", Akash said.

He further gave her a couple of pieces of advice. "I wanted to be in a perfect relationship but I was wrong. Don't repeat that mistake. I've learned a lot of it", Akash advised.

Akash was about to leave the room when Shree stopped him. And asked him about his future plans.

"Will you talk to her?", Shree asked

"I don't know but I need her", Akash replied.

"I tried to contact her but I couldn't able to approach her", she told him.

"I know, she will never forgive me. I was chasing for such a relationship that didn't even exist. These Six months have completely changed me inside out", he said.

"What will you do now?", She asked.

"I'll try to find her. I'll try to get her back in my life", he said with determination.

"And what if you didn't make it up?", She said.

"Then I'll tell my heart that Suhani was an illusion but nothing. And I can't get out of it", he said and left the room.

He didn't further need any therapist because his past mistakes and his losses changed him inside out. For him, love is nothing but an illusion and that illusion led him to the blues.

A therapist needed to help him in taking away those blues. His own mistakes and losses helped him understand that love is an illusion and that one needs to find peace in this illusion.

... (Since Rahul went to Shree's home with a proposal, they got married after three months. After the wedding, they lived in their own house and Akash used to visit them often) ...

Akash was happy for Shree and Rahul. He was happy that Shree and Rahul had so many differences but still, they were ready for a beautiful journey and got married.

"The loss of her mother and the break up with Suhani had taught you so many things, but this wedding of Rahul and Shree completely changed his perception of love," Rahul concluded,

True love is meant to last a lifetime. So, there is nothing wrong with being patient and making sure you get things right.

Now Akash was ready to go back to Suhani to get her back in his life.

CHAPTER FOURTEEN

'COME, SAIL AWAY WITH ME'

"Until You've lost your reputation, you never realize what a burden it was or what freedom is"

His plane was about to land in the city of love; Paris, capital of France. He was reading a book that he started the day before his flight. He was about to tag this book as his second favorite book, Gone With The Wind. He stopped reading it further as he was about to land. He saw the view from the window of the plane. He closed his eyes for a while and asked himself.

"Why am I here?"

"True love story never ends", he said himself.

He sighed and prepared himself to start a new chapter of his life. His whole life was running in front of him like a movie. He still can imagine that he was in Bangalore, a week ago in his house and was recalling his memories with Suhani.

He had been searching for her for the last few months.

She left her office six months ago. She left Akash's house and went away to Paris.

Many of the questions were circulating in his mind what if she had moved on? What if she got married to someone more compatible with her? All these questions were disturbing him only.

"Sir please tie your seat belt", the air hostess said.

He tied up his belt, and after a while when the plane landed, they were at the land of Paris. According to information, Suhani is living in Saint Germain and the Latin Quarter on Paris's Left Bank. It's a hub of artists and intellectuals and is crammed full of unique boutiques and cozy wine bars, not to mention some of the best brunches in Paris.

It was a perfect city for Suhani to live in. She had always talked about living in Paris.

(Akash recalled his memories with Suhani)

Paris is known for a lot of things, but perhaps the most famous is the City of Love.

Love is always in the air when you visit Paris. From history to the modern-day, Paris remains a destination for people celebrating love or looking for the alluring emotion.

Akash was also looking for the love of his life. He can't wait to see Suhani and to be with her again.

His love lust took him to a strange city. He went to the given address and looked around the people there first.

He was staring at each corner to recognize Suhani. He went inside the quarter and asked the receptionist about the room of Suhani.

"I am looking for my friend. Her name is Suhani. She has been living here. Can you tell me about her room or would you call her for me at least?", he asked the receptionist.

"Sir, your friend's full name?", She replied.

"Suhani Malhotra", he told her.

"Sir I am sorry to inform you that she checked out from here three days ago", she replied.

Akash's heart breaks into pieces, but he gathers himself and asks the receptionist about her contact number.

"Usually, we don't give personal information to any strangers, but if you want to have her contact number then you have to give some of your personal details", she said.

Akash was ready to do anything for Suhani at that moment. He gave the receptionist his personal details and got Suhani's number.

"Is there anything else I can do for you?", the receptionist asked.

"Yes, I want to book the room in which Suhani was living. Can you book that for me?", Akash emphasized.

"Sir it has already been booked, sorry I can't give you this favor", she apologized.

"It's okay, thank you", Akash said.

Akash left the building and called on the given number, but nobody received his call. His heart was sinking over time. He sat at the corner of the building and tried to make up his mind. He then decided to go to the other places as well. He took a cab and went to the love-locks bridge.

He decided to wait for Suhani there. He thought that maybe Suhani would visit this place in the evening. So, he decided to wait for her at the bridge. He was looking at the couples and recalling his memories with Suhani as a couple.

Suhani always wanted to do this tradition of love lock at the bridge. His reminiscence of the early days of his relationship with Suhani was coming in front of his eyes.

He recalled Suhani's statement from the past,

"When we will go to Paris, we will write our names on the padlock and will lock it together".

(He smiled)

The whole day, he waited for Suhani but he didn't see her anywhere. At midnight, he decided to go to the

Apartment. He booked him a room in a nearby building.

Before going to sleep, he called on Suhani's number but no one was picking up the phone. He put the phone on the side table and closed his eyes. When he was about to sleep, his phone rang. He thought that it was Suhani and he picked up his phone in a hurry to attend to the call but it was Rahul.

"Hey! Akash, how are you, my boy?", Rahul asked.

"I couldn't find her Rahul. She left the Quarter a few days ago", he told Rahul.

"Akash…", Rahul was about to say something, but Akash disconnected the call. He was crying like a baby.

He regretted his mistake. But he wiped off his tears and put together himself once again. He promised himself to visit all the renowned places there to find Suhani.

His quest for his love was no less than a trauma. In one second, he loses hope, and in the next second, he puts together himself to find her love. He was in a state of continuous pain.

The next day, he called Suhani's office mate and asked her further about Suhani.

"She wasn't there", he told her.

"It was all I could do Akash. Believe me! I have nothing else to tell you", she said

"Did she tell you about any of her relatives living in Paris?", Akash asked.

"No Akash, she didn't tell me that much", she replied

Akash disconnected the call and went outside the building. He decided to go to the Eiffel Tower. Of course, that monument is breathtaking and a sign of love. People usually spend most of their time there with their counterparts. He was determined that he would see Suhani someday. This was the reason that he didn't give up.

"Stop the car right here", he said in a hurry.

(The driver stops the cab)

Akash got out of the car and started chasing a girl. He thought that it was Suhani. He ran after her a bit and poked her on her shoulder. "Suhani!", he called her

But when the girl turned over, it wasn't Suhani. It was Akash's misunderstanding.

"I am sorry", he apologized. (He was taking breathing heavily.)

"It's okay", the stranger replied.

He went back to the cab and apologized to him too. The driver could understand his situation since he told him already that he was there to look for someone.

He gave him all of his money (the automobile rental) and sat at the Eiffel Tower's corner. He's disintegrated once more. His search for love was humiliating him to no end.

"We will be there at the top height of the city of love, and we will express our feelings with a loud voice", he recalled Suhani's desires once again.

He got up and went to the topmost height of the tower. He said aloud,

"Where are you, Suhani?"

(His eyes were full of tears)

He once again waited for the whole day and it turned out to be useless there. He said to himself,

"I just wanted to see her".

He further said, "I just wanted to see you happy Suhani".

He was so much disturbed that he fell ill. His hotel caretaker was there to take care of him a little bit.

He went asleep and had a terrible dream about Suhani. He got up and cried a lot.

He was like hell, and his heart was bleeding. Nothing was helping him out. He cried for his own mistakes.

"I should kill myself", he cried.

He wasn't ready to give up, and he didn't even want to.

He got up and went outside to take a cab, and went to the Panthéon. Suhani was a great lover of the architect. Her main reason for choosing Paris was because of its beautiful neoclassical architecture.

He was looking at every single girl with great attention. He remained vigilant all day. He was all alone in a big city and looking for the person he loved the most. He called Suhani's contact number once again, and this time someone picked up the phone. His heart skipped a beat.

Within a second, he thought that he talked to her and begged her to be with him again. His heart started beating fast.

"Hello! Suhani?", Akash said.

"Sorry?", A female replied.

"Who's there?", She further questioned.

"I am Akash, where are you?", he replied.

"Who is Akash?", Someone asked.

"Suhani ma'am is not here now. Call her later", the female said and disconnected the call.

He was in the middle of the riddle. He thought that it was Suhani's assistant. He was happy that she was able to start something on her own. He was actually happy for her.

For the next ten days, he visited many of the places and streets of Paris but he didn't find her.

He decided to leave Paris the next day because his father was all alone. He said himself,

"Not all the love stories have happy endings".

He decided to visit the love-lock bridge once again. He bought a padlock from the shop and wrote his name over there. He wrote Suhani's name as well and decided to lock it on the bridge. His heart was beating so heavily. He got the vibe that something was about to happen to him. When he arrived there, his soul had shaken so much hard that he was about to lose his senses.

"Suhani", he whispered.

He saw Suhani with another guy, locking up the padlock together. His eyes were full of tears. He couldn't help it.

He was looking at them from a distance. Unconsciously, his padlock fell from his hand, and his hands started shaking with shock. He was losing himself.

He put his hands on his mouth and cried so hard. He never cried like this, even at his mother's funeral.

He decided to go back right away because this was all he could do at that moment. With a broken heart, he went to the airport. He decided while leaving Paris that he would never forget his love for Suhani.

"At least, I was able to see her", he said to himself and sighed.

The whole moment got stuck in his mind. he can't get rid of that. His eyes filled with tears.

"I never got the chance to say I love you,

I never got the chance to say I miss you,

Nobody told me that how easy it was to remove the memories of a loved one,

It hurts! I never said Good-Bye". So many random questions were coming into his mind.

He finally left Paris because he saw his love with her love. He wasn't able to react. It was like, his soul was swooning slowly. He had missed the bullet. His mind was not ready to accept this bitter truth. His heart didn't want to leave the city because his love was living there.

He was so hurt by the very moment that he once again lost his senses at the Delhi airport.

(He was taken to the hospital by ambulance)

"Akash", his father was trying to wake him up.

Akash opened his eyes.

"Dad", he murmured.

"It's okay", his father comforted him.

Rahul and Shree came with the reports. They both looked so disappointed. Shree was trying to control herself. She had tears in her eyes.

Rahul appeared in front of Akash. He hid his reports and met him with courage.

"Yes, my brave boy is here with us again", Rahul said.

He hugged him and held his hand into his hand. "We will never leave your side", he said to Akash looking at his face.

"I want to go home", Akash whispered.

"We will be there after a while", he said.

"Get some rest", Shree said.

His reports were so devastating. They (reports) tore all of them apart. When Akash's father read the reports, he lost his hopes once again. He had his hands on his head.

Shree tried to help him in pulling himself together. They didn't want to tell Akash that he was suffering from Glioblastoma. Which is a severe type of brain tumor. Not to mention, this type of tumor is usually very aggressive, which means it spreads rapidly. Shree was crying too.

"It can't be true", Shree said

Rahul was trying to convince her to control herself.

The doctors came to visit Akash. They were trying to give them hope but they all knew that the tumor was about to cross its limit.

"You'll be fine Akash", they said.

Akash was trying to get them because he took it as just a temporary faintness. He replied,

"I am absolutely fine now"

Doctors appreciated him for his courage. But they were also trying to give him some hints that his case is critical.

Shree and Rahul were very worried for him because they knew that he already had suffered a lot.

"You have to visit the hospital two days a week," the doctor said.

"Whenever you feel any discomfort or headaches, approach us as soon as possible", the other doctor said.

Akash was trying to understand the doctor's concerns.

"Am I okay?", He asked Rahul.

Rahul said in a trembling voice, " Yes, you are".

After a few hours, they took Akash home. Akash was in a state of suspicion. He was having an idea now that they all were hiding something from him.

His father was so hopeless that he went to his room again. For him, Akash was the only thing to live a life after his wife. They took Akash to his room. Shree got something for him to eat.

"Doctors said, you have to rest as much as you can", Rahul said.

"Yes, if you need anything, call us right away", Shree further said.

Akash said, "I am fine guys".

(They both admonished him to rest more and more)

Rahul put the reports on the table to have a glass of water. Unfortunately, Rahul forgot the reports on Akash's side table. Rahul and Shree were sitting with Akash in his room. They were trying to distract him. Soon, Akash fell asleep. Rahul and Shree left the room. They already made him rest assured that they were staying at his place and if he needed anything they were here to facilitate him.

At mid-time, Akash got up to drink water. He turned on the lamp and drank some water from the bottle. He was about to take a nap when he saw his medical reports. He got alert and grabbed the reports.

He barely cried when he came to know that suffering from a Brain tumor.

(He took a deep breath)

The next day, Rahul was searching for Akash's reports and he suddenly remembered that he forgot the reports on Akash's side table. He groaned.

"What have you done Rahul? How stupid are you?" Rahul complained himself.

Meanwhile, he was telling his stupidity to Shree, and Akash came out from his room with the reports in his hands.

"Is that what you guys were hiding from me?", He asked

"Akash...", Rahul was about to say something but Akash continued in the middle of the way

"I am not a kid Rahul. You don't need to hide it from me".

"We are sorry Akash, we don't want to disturb you anymore", Shree said on behalf of Rahul.

"That's what was written for me by God, Shree", he said.

"We can't help it now. I have already accepted the mistakes I made in my past. I am now quite able to swallow this bitter pill of the Brain tumor as well", he said.

"God is a meticulous dock maker, so precise in his order that everything on earth happens in its own time, neither a minute late nor a minute early. And for everyone without exception, the clock works accurately. For each there is a time to love and time to die", he told them.

Akash sat down on the chair. He didn't react that much because he had already faced so much trauma in his life.

"Suhani has moved on", he told them.

"Did you talk to her?", Shree asked.

"Did you meet her?", Rahul asked.

"I saw her making life-long promises with his partner", he told them.

The whole moment was once again in front of him

"All right, forget about her", Rahul said in anger.

"You have so many more things to do in your life", Shree said.

"I am happy for her. All the way to Paris, I prayed just one thing. I wanted to see her happy and she is happy", he told them.

Rahul sat in front of him and said,

"She is happy. You deserve happiness too".

"You have to fight from this disease now", Shree emphasized.

(They both helped him in getting better. They were his only support because Akash was the only support of his father)

During his surgery, Akash used to spend most of his time reading and writing. However, doctors had forbidden him from taking stress and doing something that would make him tired or stressed. But he finally found peace in reading and writing stories.

He himself wrote many beautiful short stories.

He was getting better day by day because he was working on his mental health as well. He wants to work on him and learn from his past. He visited his doctors on time and continued his medications. He wanted to move on as well. He doesn't want to regret anything. Although, he accepted that his love stories were just like a sailing boat.

He decided to tell others how he had learned from his past and wanted to make them aware of all those things they needed to consider in their relationship.

Soon he got an opportunity to write articles in some of the famous newspapers of India but he preferred to talk about love. He wants to write what he feels about love.

He wrote a book "Come, sail with me". The center of his book was all about love which he personified as a Sailing Boat. He tried to convince the reader that nothing is perfect in this world. You can hardly find a perfect match in this world.

"Love is like a sailing boat. All we can do is to ask the other person to come and sail with us" This was the main idea of his book.

"It's better to sail together rather than wrecked by a heavy storm", this beautiful line was the last line of his book. He wrote the whole book by looking at his life scenarios, especially the epoch of past life. One can analyze how much he had learned from his life.

He faced so many tough times while writing the book. Since it was his first official publication, he didn't want to give up.

He worked hard both on his writing and medications. At last, he completed his book before his surgery, and he got a huge shout-out from his writing.

The beauty in his words could be seen by the expression he had used in the book. He not only talked about love but also true friendship. All of the credit goes to his best friend, Rahul. He motivated Akash and insisted on it. He was the one who took Akash back to normal.

After a month of publishing his book, Akash's health was abating. His doctors wanted him to have surgery. At that time, his condition was so bad that the surgery became mandatory. Craniotomy was not that much easy. Although Akash's medication helped him in controlling the tumor still surgery was required. It was risky too.

Before going for the surgery, Akash was talking to Shree and Rahul.

"If anything happens to me, take care of my father", he requested.

Rahul and Shree were also upset. But still, they were encouraging Akash.

"My book is one of the pure treasures. I wrote it with all my heart. Learn from that", he said.

"Life, love, friendship, and all of the relationships out there are just like a sailing boat. You can't handle it on your own. Ask others to sail it with you".

(Akash told them and went for the surgery)